STEEL ROSES

TISHA ANDREWS

STEEL ROSES

Rose never saw it or him coming. It being love and him being Diesel, a stranger who had somehow forced his way into her life. And somehow into her world.

With college and working tirelessly just to get by, Rose's only focus is becoming a renowned physician and providing a better life for her and her father. Never having any luck when it came to love, Diesel's unsettling presence in her life is not only foreign but a recipe for disaster if she dared to entertain him.

Diesel, a local mechanic, could have anyone he wanted and did over the years. Now... he wants Rose. An intoxicating hunger won't let him expel her from his every thought, every desire, to have her. He knows it's dangerous, deadly even. Especially since he's from another world called Etan, a world where history just might be repeating itself.

While Diesel struggles to play it safe, his best friend, Getty, prefers being a rebel. He's rude, reckless, and anxious to get into all kinds of trouble. Being a musician who could swoon the undergarments off a woman doesn't help... until he crosses paths with Zara, Rose's best friend. She comes with brains, beauty, attitude, and worse—a fiancé. A fiancé who might be the reason for all of their demise.

As each becomes entangled in a web of deception in their quest for love, skeletons from their pasts birth a vicious need to seek revenge born out of a scorned and forbidden lover.

 First edition, July 13, 2020. Printed in the United States of America.

Facebook Like Page: Author Tisha "Lil Drew" Andrews

Instagram: @lil_t_drew and @author_tisha_andrews

Twitter:@tisha_p12

Email: AuthorTAndrews@gmail.com

Website: https://www.authortishaandrews.com/

Forbidden~

To abstain or not entertain, neither consume what is prohibited or not allowed.

ACKNOWLEDGMENTS

To Kandice, my heartbeat on earth from heaven.
I do this all to show you that even in late in life, God is gracious enough to allow us to still live out our dreams.
Thank you for loving your mother unconditionally.
You give me strength.

To the readers, book fifteen and I'm still learning.
Thank you for your continued support and love. My first paranormal. I pray you read it, love it, and even if it wasn't my best work from what you're used to reading from me, let me know kindly in a review.
Reviews do matter.

To B. Love, thank you. Last year, I wasn't so sure of my next steps and not because I fell out of love with writing. I just didn't know if writing could sustain the emptiness I felt, the hole in my heart. Then you gave me a yes so I can work hard trying to fill up that hole again. I appreciate you.

To the Father, the creator, I thank you.
Your grace is more than sufficient.

1

"Excuse me, ma'am. You need some help?" a man in a hooded raincoat called out to Rose, tapping on the window.

The weather had been bad all day—disgustingly bad. It didn't help that it was late as she sat in her car, feeling defeated on the side of the road.

She jumped as her breath hitched in her throat, clutching her chest. He'd scared the crap out of her after working a long shift at the diner. Now here she was, stuck with a stranger, albeit one who seemed to be offering help that she didn't even ask for nor wanted near her.

Rose cursed to herself silently, remembering the nagging sound she'd heard whenever she tried to start her car for weeks. Heard it and ignored it too. She was overwhelmed as the rain offered no mercy, coming down harder. She knew, in no time, if it kept up like this, the streets would be flooded, adding something else she'd have to worry about.

She shivered, rubbing her arms up and down in between ramming her foot down on the brake as she forcefully turned the key inside of her ignition.

"Ugh, I swear I hate my life," she groaned, close to tears.

Her car had given out on her for the third time in the past six months but never in the rain. That was all it did in good old, sunny South Florida—rain and very hard at that. She could barely see. The windows quickly fogged up as the rain mercilessly beat against her car and against... the mystery man.

"Hey, I'm just trying to help. You alright in there?" he probed, her breath hitting the glass, causing a thick fog when she looked his way angrily.

She didn't care what he was trying to do. She just wanted him to leave her the fuck alone.

Why was the question she wanted to ask him and her car since this could have happened two weeks ago while she was home instead of stuck on the side of the road.

"Blue, why, baby? Why?" she whined, talking to her 1998 blue Mustang. It was the only thing she had left of her mother, and even in its current condition, Rose loved it more than she loved almost anything. "And my freaking daddy's going to kill me," she fussed lowly, punching the brake as she turned the ignition once more. "Fuck," she uttered, then took a deep breath. "Get it together, Rose. Get it to-fucking-gether."

This was her life and had been for almost four years. Unlike most twenty-two-year-olds, she spent most of her days in school majoring in biology, then late nights working at Roscoe's Diner to make ends meet.

She had two more semesters before her graduation, which only meant eight more yeas of residency since her sights were set on medical school. She didn't grow up with much, but she was smart, disciplined, and had a lot of love being raised singlehandedly by her father.

The neighborhood called him Mr. Eddie or Mr. E. He'd been raising her on his own since she was the tender age of eight, and it hadn't been easy. Mr. Eddie was a prideful man. Rose remembered those nights, dark nights with no lights on as they sat with a candle or two, eating crackers, bologna, and cheese while he told jokes.

If Mr. Eddie was known for anything else besides fixing cars and making pretty babies like Rose, he was good at making people laugh—oh, and running off those big-breasted women who figured Rose needed a mother. There was only one woman he loved, and God took her from him. He vowed he'd never love another woman like he did his wife, and he never did.

His strong will led to staying focused, taking care of Rose, from the lop-sided ponytails he put in with crooked parts to basic meals like Hamburger Helper and sandwiches. Still, Rose was the cutest thing he'd ever seen, and it helped that she didn't care what her hair looked like or what they ate. She was her father's whole heart in human form.

Learning that early on, Rose didn't get hung up on boys or the failed relationships or what she thought were relationships from high school. Most just wanted what most girls in her hood easily gave up for free—pussy, and she was more than that. Thank God for Mr. Eddie as she mean mugged the mystery man.

She decided she might as well get the lecture over with, calling and waking up her father. She knew he would fuss, but he was retired now. Still, he could have probably fixed her car weeks ago, but it was just like Rose to procrastinate. Sniffling, she dropped her head on the steering wheel, dreading to pick up her cell phone.

All she wanted was her daddy and to cry. That was it as she tried to ignore the mystery man tapping on the window.

Hearing him tap harder this time made Rose lose it, wishing she was big and strong enough to kick his ass. Too bad she wasn't, so she opted for sending him on his way as nicely as she could.

Wiping the window, she peered deeply at him before rolling it down just enough to talk to him. When she did, their eyes met, and she backed up, feeling his chocolate orbs practically pierce her to the core. *What the hell?* Rose wasn't sure what had just happened, but whatever it was scared the shit out of her. She reasoned it was fatigue coupled with aggravation, taking a deep breath as she composed herself.

"Can you just go now? Please and thank you!" she yelled at him, fighting hard not to look his way as she cried.

He looked at her, tilting his head as her voice cracked. Her eyes now pooling and spilling tears. She crossed her arms still refusing to look at him. Luckily, his body blocked the rain, but she didn't care if she got wet. She just wanted him gone.

Too bad since leaving her wasn't an option for him as he watched her pout helplessly like she had other options. In fact, it didn't matter that she fumed, having a temper tantrum. He saw past that and through her, feeling her sadness, willing her to give it to him. And he was just as stubborn as she was, giving no fucks about the rain that pounded against his body as she feverishly rolled up the window only for him to tap on it again.

"Oh, God. Why does he keep doing that?" She closed her eyes, quickly wiping her tears with the back of her hand, then silently prayed he'd just go away. That prayer, however, must have bypassed God as she looked to her left, and he was still right there.

"Look, call anyone," he yelled, pulling out his cell. "Give them my name. It's Diesel, by the way."

After he slipped his cell back in his pocket, he lifted both arms, placing them on top of the car. He was relaxed as if it were ninety degrees outside with the sun blazing down, pissing her off too.

"Too bad I'm not leaving," he told her as she furiously wiped the glass to tell him to kiss her ass, but she soon reasoned within herself that he was trying to help as the rain kept at it.

Torn and tired, Rose sighed, then asked, "What do you need me to do?"

The man she now knew as Diesel smiled. When he did, it was as if the sky opened up, revealing an iced-out grill, covering perfectly aligned teeth. She saw a hint of light flash in his eyes, and then he stopped smiling as he cleared his throat.

Who the fuck is he?

If she could, she would have cranked up her car and took off. Since she couldn't, she sat stuck as that smile and gleam in his eyes mesmerized her. Then a calm, like no other, washed over her, forcing her to focus long enough to get out of this mess she'd created.

"I got to stop drinking that damn Cuban coffee," she muttered, convinced it had to be the espressos that had her tripping, feeling the way she was feeling about a stranger.

"How about you start by popping the hood?" he said, his rich, raspy voice almost sending a vibration of sorts through her.

When it happened, she checked her own forehead, clearly not just fatigued but maybe sick now. Her skin was normal to the touch, yet she felt all warm on the inside.

"Ugh," she complained, doing what he said as he took off to the front of her car. When she did, she wiped her windshield and leaned down to look underneath the crack between the hood and dashboard, watching him stand and study her engine.

When he caught her staring, he winked, causing her to drop her head down in a panic. Luckily for him, the hood shielded some of the rain. Strangely, that made Rose feel better before she sucked her teeth.

Then he smiled again, being caught up in the paradise before him he loved to tinker with. He deemed the old-school engine paradise—eager to get his hands dirty... literally as Rose was now all in, studying him once again, then stopped as she sat back and closed her eyes.

"Rose, he's going to think you're weird as hell. Just relax... Just relax."

Still, seconds later, she was right back at it, bending down just a little to get another peek at him. He was like a magnet, pulling her in against her will and she couldn't stop it. He smiled once more when he caught her, their eyes latching on to each other. When they did, a chill traveled down her spine then up his as she fought hard to pull away.

"Thank you to the mother and father of this creation," she whispered, chewing on her already-short nails while studying the likes of this specimen playing superhero in a superhero way.

His body was thick and burly in a blue, mechanic's outfit that fit him perfectly. Short of him minding her business, Rose had no complaints with what she saw. She figured she might as well have a private drool party since she had no plans of ever seeing him again in her life once he got her car to start.

What shocked her more was him not really even being her type. She was never the popular girl growing up, and the guys that were attracted to her were more interested in her doing their homework. So she spent most of her Friday and Saturday nights at home with her father with her face in a book or watching movies.

After ten minutes of him tinkering around, Rose became impatient. She didn't know why this rain didn't drive him nuts like it did her, and she had less than six hours to be up and off to class.

"This is crazy. I just need to call my daddy," she said to herself, grabbing and tossing her jacket around her shoulders to go talk to him and send him on his way. She unlocked and opened her door, taking off toward him, squealing the entire time as the rain beat forcefully against her bare legs.

"What's up?" he asked her coolly or tried to, upset she was getting wet.

Rose peeped his attitude as he watched her tap dance and shiver. He grunted when he noticed her hair was getting wet, too. It was so fucking beautiful to him —thick coils, a few dangling around her face, causing her to look so angelic but in a sexy, naughty kind of way.

"I, uh, just didn't feel right letting you do this alone," she lied, seeing him fume as he shook his head. "And you're getting soaked?" he said, his jaw twitching when he did.. She laughed nervously, unconsciously inching his way as the rain continued to hit her body as she brushed up against his.

As she did, their eyes connected while he still worked the wrench slowly, damn near undressing her soul. She thought she heard him grunt just a little, then sniff her, making her lean back when he did. Pretending she was imagining things, she cleared her throat, then asked, "Need any help?"

"Naw," he said, licking his full lips as she tucked hers away, instantly wanting to see how his felt against hers. Silently dismissing her, which was harder the longer he felt her against him, he fought to give all of his attention to the battery cable caked up with battery acid.

"Ugh, that's so... nasty," she said, her voice trailing off as she squirmed.

"It happens when things are left unattended," he said lowly and laughed, tapping away at the acid.

She caught that, squirming all the more as her center began to moisten. Diesel rolled his neck around in an effort to ignore it, but his manhood was hard. So he stretched he legs apart just a little before pulling her in front of him to block the rain. Rose wanted to resist, but she didn't, firmly planting her small body against his.

Damn, he feels so damn good, she thought.

He chuckled, and her eyes popped wide open, wondering if she'd said that out loud. It didn't matter, not when she didn't realize that he could hear her. He could hear her thoughts and that of many others since he wasn't human.

"So when's the last time you got this cleaned?" he asked, fighting hard to stay out of her head. He genuinely wanted to help her, but he'd help himself to more if she kept that up, but he knew better. The life he now lived didn't fit the life like a woman such as Rose, shaking it off so he could be on his way. If not, Rose was getting fucked tonight right against her car's engine.

"What? My engine?" she asked, then realized she sounded like a birdbrain and acted like one, too.

He grunted once more, close to begging her to get away from him when her butt brushed against his thickened member. If she stood there any longer, he wasn't sure if he could keep his hands on the wrench or battery cable. To be small, Rose had some ass on her.

"Yeah," he forced out in a half groan. "The battery."

Then her refusal to leave, even while getting wet herself, let him know she was a person who cared about people and had a good heart. She would make anyone a good friend, but right then, he wasn't thinking "good friend" thoughts. The smell of her pussy was like candy —a candied apple if he were being specific. Sticky and oh so sweet. He gulped, imagining her pussy leaking in his mouth as he suctioned it all up.

"Your hair, it's getting wet," he somewhat whispered, fighting hard not touch it as he stared at it closely now. Smelled it, too.

"I know. It's already ruined," she confessed but not just about her hair, resuming her little dance. It was her entire next day that was coming sooner than later the longer they stayed out there, yet being there with him made it feel almost worth it.

He smiled, loving the thick texture, creating goose bumps when he imagined running his fingers through it. The little dance she did was initially cute, but all that squirming around was about to send her little ass to the moon if he put some dick in her.

"Look, if you really want to help, just take this and go chill back inside," he said with as much composure he could muster up, removing his raincoat.

Before she knew it, he'd draped it around her shoulders and pulled the hood over her head. It was huge, hanging effortlessly past Rose's knees, and it smelled like him—a woody, forest scent.

Delicious, she thought.

"When you get back inside, try cranking up the car, please," he told her and smiled.

He never thought a man could smell delicious, but he'd take that. She noted he sounded frustrated when a bolt of lightning shot through the sky. Soon, a large boom was heard, and Rose was now in his arms, her face against his massive chest.

"Oh my God!" she gasped, her body shivering against his.

Immediately, his left arm became the only thing keeping her from falling while he fell for her instead... and hard. Their energies intertwined as one as both refuse to let go. She was breathtaking to Diesel, snatching every ounce of breath from his lungs that he gladly gave to her.

He felt her soul shaking while his shook in return, eager to know her as he inhaled her scent once more, but this time, it was in his system. Unknowingly, she managed to do something he vowed no woman would ever do again *ever.*

When she finally pulled away, the streetlights nearby exposed her penny-colored skin. There wasn't a blemish in sight, and when she opened her mouth, the small gap between her teeth was the icing on the cake. Diesel wanted her, and now.

He clenched his jaw, fighting hard to be the gentleman he was raised to be in spite of how he did most women. The ones he deemed as a casual fuck knew a different Diesel, a more vulgar and savage side of him. As her petite body effortlessly fit the frame against his larger one… it was damn near perfect, too perfect.

"I—I'm so sorry," she said, patting the side of his arm for him to release her. He loosened his hold, but he couldn't let Rose go just yet. Not when she felt just right in the space she was in with him..

"You're okay now?" he asked instead, even though he was far from being okay.

"Ye—Yeah, I think so. I think I should go now," she suggested, although he felt her struggling with what to say.

When she rapidly blinked her huge, brown orbs, he wanted to rest in them, frustrated once she peeled his arm from around her back.

"Yeah, good idea," he whispered, studying her, smelling her. *What the fuck is really going on?* he asked himself.

"Okay, bye," she yelled over the rain, backing up just a little but still there.

Please go, he begged her silently.

By now, he felt his insides churning and his thoughts spiraling out of control. The connection was almost unnerving as this stranger, this small human, seemed to control all of his faculties. As if she heard him, she jetted off quickly and hopped back into her car. When she slammed the door, he could have sworn he heard her locking it.

"Fuck," he groaned, taking a deep breath. The crazy thing was no lock could stop him if he wanted her, and he did want her really bad. "D, get it together," he told himself. "You can do this. The fuck is wrong with you?" When he peered down, underneath the hood her way, there she was staring like he was a movie. Her eyes were affixed on him as she vigorously wiped the windshield.

He quickly looked down and busied himself, knocking off the rest of the battery acid. Once he did, he still couldn't, however, get the battery cable off. He was sure that was what it was, rigorously shaking the cable to loosen it up some.

From the looks of the engine, it had seen better days, but to him, it was a classic. Just not given the right attention like he implied to her, like his heart. When he was done, he bent down and yelled, "Crank it up now!"

By now, he couldn't see as the fog reappeared. Still, he knew she heard him when he heard a slow, churning sound, and then a click.

"Again?" she yelled.

"Wait a second," he said lowly, holding his finger up. He knew she understood since she didn't right away.

She swiftly wiped the fog and leaned down, watching him fiddle around with the cable once more. His hands were huge and fast. Very fast. She swallowed hard, imagining just how strong he was, eyeing the prominent veins in his arms, causing her to squirm even more as he wiggled the wrench a few times. Then his mouth—oh, his mouth was even better as he bit down on his lower lip, then tucked them both in.

"God, can I be a whole hoe tonight?" she asked herself, taking a deep breath.

And if she even thought about asking her best friend, Zara, what she should do, the answer would be "hell yeah". It was always "hell yeah" when it came to Zara. She was the free, sexual being out of the two of them, equally smart and a pre-med student just like Rose.

Rose had no clue just how powerful a woman's parts could be until she met Zara. From waxes to vaginal steams, Zara worshipped hers, and her fiancé seemed to worship it, too. Rose just had no one to test this powerfulness with, so she sat around, indulging and listening to Zara.

Zara even gave hers a name. She called hers Wonderland. Said it was better than then an amusement park, filled with rides on end and good things to eat.

"Let me grab my truck and pull it around!" he told her, jogging to a truck she'd just noticed across the street. It was an old, flatbed truck with some wording on the side.

Whipping it around, he put it in park and hopped out, leaving it running. After connecting what she assumed were jumper cables from his truck to her car, he yelled, "Try now!"

The slow, churning started again. It kept going and going as he started to smile, his teeth making her tighten her thighs. Then, out of nowhere, the engine roared.

"Give it some more gas!"

She did, and it roared once more.

Then it stopped.

"Oh no. What happened?" she whispered to herself, her excitement quickly dissipating. It was close to two in the morning now.

Instead of asking her to try again, Diesel pushed down the hood, then headed her way casually as if he'd fixed the problem. When she wiped the fog, she saw him motioning for her to roll the window down. Rose mouthed *why* as he grunted, shaking his head.

"Can you just roll it down, please?" he finally asked her, that rasp soliciting her will to give in.

She did but only cracked it, being her stubborn self once again. Instead of fussing, he chuckled, his iced-out teeth appearing that took her breath away. At this point, anything she did was amusing to him. Even being stubborn, although it was his choice to be soaked when he stopped to assist a total stranger.

Catching her frustration as he stared at her, he quickly dropped the smile. "It's the alternator. I had to remove the left cable to see if it was just the battery and all that other sh—I mean, acid you had on there. When's the last time you cleaned it?"

"Cleaned what?" she asked as if she didn't watch him chip all that gunk off of her battery, close to tears again.

"The battery," he said, grinning again as he dragged his hand down his face. When he was done, he tucked his lips, the same ones that had Rose squirming, and she got stuck. "Listen up," he said, snapping her out of her haze. "I need you to get your stuff. Then lock it up over here so I can take you home. Tomorrow, I'll send one of my boys through here to grab your car. And no worries, it's on me."

Rose gawked hearing that. She had all of fifty bucks to her name to get her through to next week. Half of that was for gas, and the other was for a few food and toiletry items.

"Thanks, but no thanks," she said nastily, rolling up her window all the way up. She was about to activate plan B, and that was to call Zara. She saw Diesel's patience, which was growing thin. He hated what he had to do next, but she pushed him.

He grinned, showing his sexy ass smile, then played unfairly with what he did next.

You're going to trust me, let me take you home, and fix your car. You will be okay with letting me do it, too, since I'm not waiting for a fucking friend. Fuck that. I'm here.

The entire time he controlled her mind, taking

control over, Rose was tuned in to him, noticing his eyes. They were the color of maple syrup. She liked that—them, along with his rich, mocha-colored skin.

"I'll let you know once it's done and whether you're paying or not," he told her, putting his foot down. "Now, lock it, and let's make a move."

"Fine," she huffed, instantly agreeing as she grabbed her keys out of the ignition before locking and closing the door.

"About time. I swear I'm close to swimming out here, ma," he teased her as if he hadn't done what he'd just done to get her to agree.

When he backed up, she took note of his thick thighs and bowed legs. Even under his mechanic jumpsuit, he looked good. Tonight was such a crazy but eventful night, making her smile.

"This damn girl," he mumbled as she followed him to his truck. "Give me the keys, and here's my cell," he said, this time handing it to her as he grabbed her book bag. "It's heavy, almost bigger than you," he told her, answering her question before she asked what he was talking about. He had a bad habit of that when something had all of his attention, revealing shit he just shouldn't know. "You can put in your address in the GPS."

Still, she did as he instructed, stomping behind him as she fiddled with his cell.

"Oh, I have nothing to hide, so scroll away," he told

her, chuckling as he opened the door for her to get in. Once she was in, he quickly went around and hopped in, feeling the water run down in his seat. "Shit, I am really wet."

I am, too. Very wet, she thought, crossing her legs at her ankles. He shot her a look yet said nothing as before he reached behind her and grabbed a clean towel.

"Here, use this."

Before she could protest, he was reaching behind her again, grabbing one for himself. He was practically on top of her, his wood-scented smell invading her nose as he reached over and pulled the seat belt across her chest.

"Oh." She flinched, then laughed, feeling like a big ball of nerves.

"Relax. Just buckling you in. Truck's old and sometimes this here belt gives people a hard time," he said with a wink.

"Yeah, I bet it does," she said, recovering as she cleared her throat. "Thank you."

"You're welcome. Now, where to since you haven't put that address in?" he said as she tried to get her thoughts together but couldn't. She also noticed his hands were rugged and calloused but shuddered, remembering how they felt against her body.

"Oh, yeah right," she said and laughed, feeling stupid. "My address."

"Diesel," he said. "And then call your friend to tell

her. You know how you girls call your friends to tell them about some guy you ended up with."

"If I did make a call, who said it would be to a girl?" she sassed back.

"That broken down car," he told her, a sly grin resting on his face that made her melt.

Rose knew right then he was going to be hell to deal with until she got her car back.

"Dude a lame if he is your man," he said, grunting the more he thought about her having a man. *A fucking lame.*

2

"And that's a nice name. Diesel, like the gas," she said, kind of prissily, and he chuckled instead of offering hers.

She didn't have to, though. He already knew it. Saw it on her nametag. Still, he wanted her to tell him like most women did.

Honestly, he was used to hood chicks—the loud, boisterous, and aggressive kind. He could tell she had a little feistiness to her, but baby girl wasn't playing around with her life. That book bag, coupled with that diner uniform she had on, told him she had more goals than dating and random hookups.

Once the address was in, he looked over and said, "Sit back, baby girl. I got you." She just didn't know how much he really did, but in time, she would know.

Once they pulled up to her spot, he looked over and

grinned. Rose was knocked out, even mumbled a few times like she was still fussing at him. Instead of startling her, he sat for a few minutes, inhaling her scent, smelling the slickness between her legs even more.

In awe she was turned on by him as he was with her and this wasn't even about sex. It was about them—their connection. He took a deep breath, loving the smell of pussy -- clean pussy -- like Rose's. She smelled as if she hadn't been out and about all day at work.

As if she felt him staring, undressing her with his mind, and tasting her essence, she shot up and looked his way, then at her apartment building. "Oh, we're here," she mumbled, stretching as she yawned and sat up, adjusting her eyes, which landed on his.

"Just pulled up. I didn't want to wake you."

Wish I could wake up to you and those fucking eyes. Fine ass.

It didn't matter that Rose was smaller, leaner than what he was used to. She was just right... for him.

"Uh, okay," she said, rubbing her eyes as she sighed. She was so tired but grateful as a sheepish grin was plastered on her face, feeling his orbs bore into hers.

"So tomorrow?" she asked, feeling warm as she shifted in her seat, eager to get out due to the stickiness between her thighs. She was embarrassed, but he was enthralled.

"Yeah, I'll get with you tomorrow, but what's your name, and how will I call you?" he asked instead, ready for her to leave before changed his mind about letting her. She gasped, then laughed, converting into a snort. Now she was really embarrassed.

"Really?" he asked, cracking up.

"I know, I snort sometimes when I laugh, but I'm tired and it's Rose," she said, her name tickling his ear when she said it.

"I mess with that. So Rose what?" he slid in, wanting to hear her say her whole name.

"Rose Steel," she said, looking away as she grinned. *Gosh, I like him.* She knew a guy like him wasn't single but it didn't mean she couldn't like what she saw. "Oh, here's your raincoat," she said, unveiling it from her body.

"That's what's up, Rose Steel. And keep that. I'm going to need you to take better care of yourself," he told her, gazing her way as he felt that churning again he'd never experienced before.

This is fucking nuts, he told himself.

It is. D, what the hell is wrong with you? Don't. Just don't, D. She's a fucking human. A human, human. Cute, but I already can see she's going to be a problem. That was Getty, his best friend, talking.

All Etans could do it if you let them in, but Getty bullied his way in when it came to Diesel. That was more than his best friend. He was his brother. All their lives, they were attached at the hip, but what made Getty cling to Diesel more was he was part human, born of a human mother. That made Diesel question his value, but it was Diesel's connection to humans that led to him being torn between worlds, forcing Getty to follow him to Earth where they both lived now.

It wasn't forbidden, but it wasn't Etan, making Getty low key despise human woman when it came to his best friend. Especially since one in the past hurt him deeply.

Fuck you, G. Fuck you, Diesel told him, biting his lip as he looked at Rose.

3

By the time Rose made it up two flights of stairs soaking wet, she had just enough energy to pull off her clothes and shower before sleep found her quickly again. She felt like she tossed and turned all night, even though must of the night had passed. When the alarm went off at six a.m., it scared the shit out of her as she looked around, ready to cry.

"Ugh!" she huffed, her body feeling like a block of lead.

It only got worse when she remembered she didn't have her car. She hit the snooze button, wanting to reset her life as the five minutes zipped by before the alarm rang once more.

"Get up, Rose," she grumbled to herself.

Since she had to take the bus, she had just enough time to get dressed, make a cup of coffee, and do something quick to her hair. Scurrying out of bed, she ran to the bathroom, sped through her facial regimen of an oatmeal and apple facial scrub, then brushed her teeth. She loved facial scrubs, often only splurging on them, obsessed with not getting acne. As a teen, acne was also another reason she sucked at dating, so anything to keep that at bay was worth the splurge.

Running quickly to her closet, she grabbed and slipped on a pair of khaki slacks, a white button-up top, then removed her last clean lab coat. After putting on the denim sneakers she loved so much, she snatched her satin scarf off of her head and ran her fingers through her hair.

It was in dire need of a perm, and the rain didn't help it at all. The curls that formed were now mashed against her head from sleep. With no money to spare, she pulled out a huge tub of hair gel, swiftly grabbing a glob of it as she worked it through. It took some time to do this when her hair was dry. She grunted the entire time until it was all detangled.

Grabbing a few ponytail holders, she pushed her hair back, then rigorously worked her brush until her hair behaved, laying down nicely against her scalp. A quick braid with a few bobby bins to tuck the loose hair, and Rose was ready to go.

She knew her funds weren't in the best shape now, so this would have to do. And Zara actually thought she was the cutest when she wore her natural hair. She always called her a liar since Zara did what best friends should do—lie and make you feel better. Well, at least that was what she thought. She then moisturized her skin, wiping her eyebrows as she smoothed them down.

"Girl, you really need a serious spa and salon day," she said to herself and frowned. "And that won't be happening until about," she sang, looking at her watch, "at least eight to ten years."

She sighed, then looked up, wrinkling her nose. She wished it were full, instead of short and pointy like her mother's, to give her face some roundness, but it was the only thing she had from her mother, so she embraced it. The rest of her was all her father, from her short frame, large, round eyes, and cheekbones to her skinny legs. Then she heard a series of knocks on her door, startling her.

"What the hell?" she spat, looking in the mirror before she stuck her head out of her bedroom door. She walked down her hallway slowly, totally perplexed. Most burglars or robbers didn't knock, but shit happened. This was the hood.

She eased into the living room, then went behind her sofa to grab her bat. She was terrified of guns, but she'd rock a skull or two with her steel bat if she had to. Then they knocked again, riling her up even more.

"Who is it?" she yelled, practicing as she swung her bat behind the door. "I got a mean swing for you," she whispered, then yelled, "I have a bat! And I know how to use it!"

She heard a loud laughed, freezing up when he said, "Rose, really? Put the bat down. It's me, Diesel."

"What the hell is he doing here," she fussed before she dropped the bat on her foot, and hard. "Ouchhhh!"

"Rose? Rose!" he shouted, banging harder on her door. "Rose, let me in!"

She hopped on her good foot, cursing to herself while he banged like a maniac. She wished it was his head she'd hit and was close to tears as her foot throbbed with pain. Standing unsteadily as she prepared to curse him out, she unlocked the door and gave him a menacing stare. But even through that, Diesel saw the pain etched on her face, but more importantly, he felt it too.

"What is it?" she growled, looking so cute to him, then stopped when the pain she felt hit his foot that he began to wiggled.

"You hit your foot, Rose?" he asked, his face full of concern. She thought he was being funny, about to close the door when he grabbed it and pushed his way in.

"Ouchhhh. Do you even sleep?" she groaned as she held on to the door, hopping back a step or two.

"I do," was all he said before he had his way with her, swopping her up in his arms. "Here, let me," he said before she could contest it, placing her gently on a nearby chair before he removed his arms from underneath her.

The fresh smell of soap sprung up in the air, landing subtly in her nose. That wood smell too. And he looked good, damn good too. The night light didn't do him any justice as she fussed at her center, responding to him once more.

God, he still smells delicious, she thought as she inhaled his scent, almost forgetting about her foot.

Her heightened sense of smell most days annoyed people, but now, it fascinated her as she sniffed him without her even knowing it. Diesel smiled but said nothing as he moved slowly toward her foot.

This girl has a thing with smells, too, he though to himself.

He watched her dangling her foot, moving it with caution as she watched his every move close to whimpering.

"I'm not trying to hurt you, Rose," he told her, feeling her anxiety shoot throughout his body.

Still, she winced before he touched it, making him chuckle.

"Rose, I haven't even touched you yet." *Even though I fucking want to.*

"I know," she whined while tears began to pool up in her eyes. "It just hurts."

"As it should. You dropped a bat on it," he told her,

giving her a cute "duh" look. "I just want to see it. I need to know if it's broken."

Rose didn't know it, but Diesel, unfortunately, could feel the pain and discomfort of others. It was something he discovered as a child, often running to help birds with broken wings or dogs injured when hit by a car. His mother thought he had a fascination with animals, but it was their pain, their discomfort, that seemed to draw him in.

Soon, it was people. He managed, over the years, not to become overwhelmed, but not feeling meant he became something he didn't want to be—insensitive. Feeling made things matter to him, and right now, everything about Rose mattered. And it didn't help that he was a hopeless empath when it came to people he loved...

I can't. Not again. I fucking can't.

Unlike the other Etans, people from his world, he saw value in humans, but humans sometimes disturbed him, being part human himself. Many were selfish and greedy and lacked morals. To the Etans who lived amongst them, that was a weakness. If asked, he would tell you Etans were arrogant fucks, but it came with the territory—the territory of being one of them.

And the last time he tried to love, it was a human who almost made him lose himself and exposed the world of Etan.

After delicately untying her sneaker, he slowly

pulled it off and then her sock. *Shit, she smells heavenly.* He grunted, then cleared his throat, this time smelling the scent of oatmeal and apple on her face from earlier. Rose was like a garden to him, smells popping up everywhere, exciting all of his senses. He closed his eyes and inhaled, then opened them quickly before he weirded her out.

"Hey, you okay?" she probed, now concerned about him. The dance between the two was crazy, but he learned quickly that whatever it was, was real and the reason he was back so soon.

"Me? I'm good," he said, shrugging her inquiry off. "It's *you* that's not okay. Now sit still," he told her, getting the attention off of him.

"You sure are bossy," she grumbled, wiping her eyes with the back of her hand.

"Here," he said, reaching for small hand towel he had in his back pocket. It was hard to ignore anything about Rose with all of her emotions running throughout his body.

What is he? The towel man, she thought and snickered to herself, taking it. He shook his head, fighting hard not to respond. Unfortunately, no matter how hard he tried, he couldn't turn Rose's thoughts off. He had it bad already.

"Now, I just want to touch it here and then here," he said, pointing to two bluish-green areas while her heel rested in the palm of his hand.

"But what if it hurts more?" she whined, tucking her lips. She dabbed her eyes once more, sniffling.

He couldn't believe a pre-med student was this sensitive. In response, he shook his head and smiled, but not for long, feeling the warmth and softness of her foot. It felt better than good. It was smooth, very smooth like baby skin.

"Well?"

"From the looks of it, some bruising. So I take it some swelling will start soon, but I don't think it's broken."

"It can't be. Why is all of this happening to me?" she cried, blowing her nose.

He couldn't help himself any longer, pinching her cheek before he slid his index finger under her chin.

"Hey, Doctor Steel. No crying. Too cute for that."

"Whatever," she mumbled, then flinched a little when he stroked her face with the pad of his thumb.

Diesel closed his eyes, feeling her struggle with his presence but not for long as he felt her nerve endings relax. When they did, he slowly and carefully began to rub her foot. Rubbed it so good that she wished he was rubbing her pussy. He did, too, as he worked a good rub in on her foot, watching and feeling her body expel with euphoria. When she came down, looking around and then down at him, she realized that pain had subsided.

"Hmmm," she said more to herself as his rough

fingers felt almost too soothing while he massaged the top of her foot some more.

He pulled back, not wanting to make things uncomfortable. He was already fucking up big time, trying to gain his own bearings as he lowered her foot. When he did, she cut her eyes at him as she rolled her foot around in circles.

He groaned inwardly as she didn't have an inkling of a clue as to how worked up she had him now. Whatever this pull was she had on him wasn't healthy. He knew it wasn't, yet he wasn't going anywhere, unless she put him out.

"It's funny. You know it still hurts, but it's not as bad as it was at first. That's so strange. Isn't it?"

"Is it? Hmmm," he replied as he examined the bluish-green mark that was now a few shades lighter. He touched it lightly, watching it lighten up just a little more before he stopped.

"Wow, that didn't hurt at all," she said as her confused look met his distressed one.

"Probably the adrenaline rush numbing it," he rationalized nervously with a chuckle, standing up. "But it's definitely bruised. I think you need a day or so off from standing on it."

Damn. I want her. I want her so bad.

He imagined lifting her leg and sticking each toe in her mouth. Sucking, licking, and devouring them for as long as she'd let him. He thought last night was just him being tired, overdoing it and not resting. Even the Etans needed time to rest and release—some through the use of their gifts, be it for the greater good or not and others through more selfish means that were self-centered yet satisfying, like fucking. But he didn't want to just fuck her. He wanted to be one with her... a human. A mere mortal human *again*.

Fuck my life.

"No, no. Oh, hell no, I can't." She quickly disputed. When she did, she tried to stand, only to sit back down as the pain shot through her foot. "Ugh," she fussed, then hissed.

"Exactly," he said, then gave her a look saying, "I told you so."

She gave him a look but not for long, immediately explaining her position. "Look, it's almost midterms. I *have* to be in class. I got this chemistry final that's a prerequisite for this class I need. Then—" she said, panicking when the stranger danger signal finally kicked in. "Wait, why are you even here?"

He snickered, knowing Rose would be the death of him if she were moving like that.

"You're just asking me that *now*?" he asked, his brows deeply knitted. He wanted to pick her up and turn her over, spanking her ass. He wasn't sure how she survived all these years, but he wasn't having it, especially with the part of town she lived in.

On his way there, he passed at least three criminals

looking to rob an innocent person such as herself and one rapist. Unfortunately, he could feel evilness lurking and prowling as well. Unbeknownst to her, he took care of them. He didn't consider himself a murderer—just someone ridding the world of evil shit. When he thought of Rose, he acted off of impulse, making sure her path would never cross the likes of them.

In fact, when he first learned how to use his powers, he was taught he could kill but only to preserve life for the greater good. Still, living amongst humans, he struggled with wanting to fit in more, understanding them instead of using what he had against them. It got lonely more and more as the years went by with him trying to find a balance. Either he secluded himself, pushing those who loved him out, or he threw himself full throttle into situations that usually didn't mean him any good.

Then he looked down at Rose and it all made sense. Humans were complicated, but it spoke to their uniqueness. And with Rose, it was like finding a little kitten he wanted to play with, watching her pout. Kittens could easily annoy you, but this kind of annoyance he yearned for. She needed him and he realized that he needed her, too.

"Yes, I'm asking you that now. Did you forget I dropped a bat on my foot?" she snapped, frustrated.

"Nope, and that's why you need a day or so to rest," he said firmly as she crossed her arms.

Diesel, bruh? Are you serious? Run, man. Get the hell out of here. There was Getty again, babysitting him. He hated to do it, but he did, blocking Getty out so he could give all of his attention back to Rose.

"I—I do, but with five classes and work, I just can't. Am I making any sense to you now?"

"Naw, you're not," he said, slipping his way inside of her head like he did the night before. She asked for it, too, being what he learned was her usual stubborn self. *You're trying to be responsible. Very responsible. It happens, but you must take care of yourself. So what you're going to do is let me take you to get your foot checked out, call off from work, and stay home from school a few days. Trust me, your professors will let you make it up. Your boss is very understanding.*

"You know what. That all can wait. My foot comes first," she said, looking and agreeing with him with ease. "I will just hit my professors up. They will let me make it up, and my boss is very understanding," she said proudly as if she came up with that responsible decision all on her own.

"And?" he said, waiting for her to repeat the rest of it about her letting him help again.

"I'm going to let you take me to get my foot checked out. Yup, that's what I'm going to do."

The last he wanted to do was to play with her mind or manipulate it, but she forced his hand, so he had no choice. That, and he wanted to have a reason to be around her. He just couldn't stop thinking about her, studying her smell, movements, the way she felt, and all like he was a machine.

He decided to shoot his boys at the shop a text, letting them know he'd be in there later today. For now, he had a date with a feisty, alluring, and humorous, in a sort of weird way, pre-med student, who had him breaking all the rules. He was ready to be that bitch nigga for her, throwing caution to the wind.

Pick your eyes up. I need to see them. And she did and smiled.

"You ready?" she asked, extending her hand for him to pick her up. He eagerly took her hand, then lifted her up.

"Oh, you gotta grab my purse and key to lock the door."

"And now you're the bossy one," he teased. "Little and bossy," he said, fighting hard to contain his excitement now that he tricked her.

When she wrapped her arms around his neck, he felt like her heart was touching his. It was like an old Etan tale about this woman called Blue Moon. Whenever the moon turned blue in Etan, it was said that love was lurking, looking for a place to land.

Focus, man. Focus.

4

"Sprained?" Rose squawked in disbelief.

"Sprained."

"Sprained?" Rose asked again, looking at Diesel and then the ER physician, Dr. Stein.

"Forgive her," Diesel interjected. "She's had a rough night," he said, clearing his throat.

"Are you sure it was just you dropping something on your foot? You seem a little out of it." The doctor grabbed the chart, checking her vitals.

Her pregnancy test was negative, and her blood work seemed normal, short of her being anemic and her vitamin D being a little low.

Diesel frowned, feeling her distress spike. She was a small, tight bundle of nerves. He could tell she was stressed in general, having a heavy school and work schedule, but something else was off.

Leave her be, Diesel.

I thought I got rid of you today.

You did, but she's got you tripping, bruh. You slipped, and I'm back now.

Before Getty had a chance to ruin his mood even more, he'd blocked him again. "Fucking annoying ass," he mumbled.

"What?" Rose asked him, confused.

"Nothing. I was thinking about someone else," he said. Rose wasn't sure if she liked that answer, but she'd take it for now. She had other problems, like her foot wrapped up with mandatory bed rest for the next week. "So Doc, her iron and vitamin D are low?" he probed, feeling Getty trying to get back in.

He made a promise to himself to fuck him up real good as soon as he saw him. They weren't equal in gifts, but in their own way, each did thrive on those that seemed to work in their favor, both coming from the Solar faction. They could do things like disappear, move objects with their minds, and hear thoughts as a few examples.

But Diesel had one thing that no other Solar had. One thing that made him stand out, and that was his ability to heal others. No one really spoke on it since it was like a secret, and it was. Only Diesel and Getty's family knew of it since their fathers were best friends, too. And, naturally, they ensured their sons grew up together thick as thieves.

Getty was a showoff as soon as he could walk, making sure he was the center of attention. He used his gifts to wow women and bag them, only to leave them clueless as he wiped their memories clear. At least on Earth, he did. He also enjoyed that he could disappear whenever he wanted, but his greatest gift was that of music.

When he played, he could lure you in, bring you to your knees, and even kill you. He was deadly with any instrument, but his instrument of choice was the guitar. He was the pretty boy of Etan, eccentric in his looks and ways. He could put Prince to shame, and on Earth, he sold out every show he performed.

Diesel resorted to the more humane, humble approach. He didn't listen to the naysayers about his human lineage, even if it was that side that almost destroyed him as he thought of Delilah, his first love.

He knew that was why Getty was on him so hard. Fuck Delilah. She was the devil herself, an unspoken topic, an ugly reminder that even though he was powerful in many ways, that four-letter word called *love* was a motherfucker. He didn't want to think about how that all ended, grabbing Rose's purse instead.

"Doctor Stein, are we almost done?"

It was close to ten o'clock by now. He had a few errands to run before going to the shop to fix her car. He got up bright and early to move it himself and not by towing it. She was already bummed about her foot, so fixing her car would be one less problem she had to mentally wrestle with.

"Yes, of course. Rose, here's your prescription for pain, and no standing for any length of time short of showering for at least for a week. Oh, and get some iron and vitamin D. Over the counter is fine. Just ask the pharmacist. Keep your foot wrapped, but make an appointment with your primary as soon as possible." Dr. Stein extended his hand to Diesel and smiled. "Watch her. I can tell she heard nothing I said," he told him, patting him on his shoulder. "Women," he whispered in his ear. "Oh, and don't forget the crutches."

"I heard that."

"Un huh. Hey, appreciate it, Dr. Stein. Thanks again," he said, shaking the doctor's hand. "Rose?" he said, reaching for her hand.

She wanted to snatch it from him, but feeling a warm jolt made her shut up as he helped her down. "Whoa," she said, the warmth buzzing inside of her.

"A little light-headed?" he asked her.

"She might be. The iron. Let me get a wheelchair," he said.

"No thanks. I got it," she said, not used to having this kind of help in her life. Especially if it wasn't Mr. Ed.

"She's got it," Diesel said to Dr. Stein, who gave him a look like "I told you so" when it came to women. After helping her place one crutch under each arm, they were ready to go.

"I need to call my professors and my job. Oh, and my daddy and Zara," she rambled on, fighting with how to turn the crutches as the made a right to head toward the elevators.

"Rose, please?" Diesel said and sighed. "Go slow."

She's going to have me acting a fucking ass about her, but I would do it all over again just to be near her. And he would.

She rolled her eyes, hearing the frustration in his voice. "I am going slow."

"Well, slower," he told her.

They heard an old lady say, "Don't they make such a cute couple? Fussing because they love each other."

Rose snorted and said, "Imagine that. Us a couple?"

"What's wrong with that?" he asked, giving her a look why that couldn't be possible.

"I'm just saying, why would you want me? I'm clumsy, broke, and probably will be for a long time. Medical school is expensive, and it takes years."

I have a lifetime, Rose. So chill.

"That's not a reason, but let's just start with me getting you to the elevator," he suggested out loud and grinned, looking down.

His iced-out teeth made her smile. Her gap made him feel like a bitch inside, wanting to see it more. He wasn't sure what she was doing to him, but he wasn't letting her shut him out, no matter what she did or said. Flaws created a uniqueness he'd come to appreciate. Even his own.

"Well, thanks. A cripple like me needs it."

"Rose, stop doing that," he warned her, getting frustrating. "I told you last night, I got you."

"Do you?" she stopped and asked.

He nodded his head, then pinched her cheek. "On this," he said, pinching her cheek once more. He noticed each time he did it, her heart fluttered and she smiled, so did his as he tucked his lip. Feeling everything she felt was making him go crazy, but in a good way..

"Good," she said lowly, giving him a goofy grin. "Race me to the elevator?"

"I'll race you alright, crazy girl."

"Oh, I'm crazy too?" she sassed, shooting him a look.

I don't care if you are. I'm crazy about you.

"Hush it," he told her as he held her lower back, motioning for her to walk. With each swing, he held his breath until her good foot landed firmly with ease on the floor.

And for the first time in years, Diesel felt at peace... with a woman. A human woman.

.

5

"Mmmmm, Hugh. Oh, God, oh God, oh, God! Yessss!" Zara squealed, hoping her fiancé hurried up.

He was humping and sweating as if he were running a marathon, but she was convinced it had to be in his head. With his rather-small member, Hugh bounced around inside of her, hitting nothing while aggravating her at the same time.

"Oh, Zara, baby. You feel so good," he grunted, humping one last time before releasing himself inside of his condom.

"Oh, yes, Hugh. You, too." She lied, rolling her eyes as she looked up at the ceiling.

She couldn't believe God had given this rather handsome and sexy man the smallest penis known to mankind. To others, Hugh Baldwin was a great catch. A top graduate of his class at Harvard and one of the most renowned oncologists in the country, treating cancer patients.

Many admired him, including her parents, after he successfully treated her mother's breast cancer. She was five years in remission, and, in her eyes, Hugh could do no wrong.

Once they learned of their daughter's interest in becoming a doctor, her parents wasted no time inviting him over for dinner. He was charming and definitely marriage material, but Zara wanted more, starting with more girth and length. To her, he was a lazy, unrewarding fuck, and she wasn't sure how much longer she could fake this.

"Damn, Zara. I can't wait to call you my wife," he told her, kissing the crook of her neck as he played in her wetness.

Zara wanted him to keep going, but she knew he wouldn't. Once Hugh came, it was over after that. She wished he gave her head instead since his head game was amazingly exquisite.

"Hugh, baby. I need you to suck your pussy," she groaned, and he smiled surprisingly—maybe because she said it *his* pussy—as he nodded his head yes.

While his tongue took her on the ride of her life, Zara tried to chase a very much-needed release. Unlike Rose, who hadn't had sex in years, Zara was a sexual animal. To her, sex was a vital part of feeling like a woman, and short of cheating, she made sure she felt like a woman, from bullets and vibrators to dildos of all colors, shapes, and sizes.

If they made it, Zara bought it and had used it at least once or twice a day since meeting Hugh. Only Rose knew of her secret play stash, thinking about her anal beads she wished she secretly tucked inside of her ass which made her orgasms just that more intense. When she did, it drove her insane while Hugh thanked himself for giving her a high he was incapable of giving when he dicked her down.

As he delicately sucked and pulled on her blooming flower, Zara felt her body give way, jerking with each tug and suck.

"Hughhhh... oh, Hugh," she moaned as he lifted her bottom, sliding his tongue deep into her anal region. "Mmmmm, suck your good pussy. This is all yours, shit." She purposefully gave ownership to him to ensure she got a bigger payoff, and it worked every time.

"I love you, Zara," he mumbled, circling his tongue around, then up and down her folds, her juices leaking and seeping into his mouth.

Her response was her dancing all over his face while he savagely licked and sucked as she came all over his face and tongue.

"Shit," she hissed, then smiled as the waves subsided, leaving her fatigued. "That was good."

"It was," he replied, wiping his mouth before he

hopped up. He quickly ran to the sink, gargling to cleanse his mouth.

She frowned when she heard that. He was the only man that treated sex like it was something he needed to scrub away as if he were in a hospital operating room.

"Zara?" he called out to her. "I gotta go in early. Can you pull out my clothes and make me some breakfast? You know, the blueberry muffins I love so much?"

"Uh, okay!" she yelled, then punched the mattress that cradled her worn-out body. She was more mentally tired than anything, shaking her head as she squinted her eyes. "Such a lame," she mumbled as she crossed her arms. She closed her eyes, wishing she was anywhere but there.

Then *it* happened. A cool air swooped in, hovering over her before resting over her body. As soon as it did, the air turned warm, and she couldn't move. Strangely, she wasn't alarmed, but what happened next was something she could never explain.

Feeling like she was floating, Zara's legs slowly rose, and her butt cheeks were gently separated. Like the plucking of guitar strings, Zara felt her body unravel in a manner she'd never felt before. She couldn't stop it, but she didn't want to. It was the best feeling she'd ever felt. Her stomach contracted wildly against her will. She couldn't think or speak. She could only feel, and boy did she feel it.

"Ahhh," she exhaled loudly, feeling her nipples

harden under a touch that felt like twisting and pinching. "Fuck!" she exclaimed, never wanting it to stop. "Keep going," she said to no one in particular. But once she did, that same lower hole that Hugh just pleased had stretched, sanctioning her to stretch her legs even wider.

As Hugh sang in the shower, Zara sang to the unsolicited presence that now held her body hostage. It was indeed divine, in an insane type of way. Her ladylove box had died and gone to heaven.

"Baby, are you trying to go there and sing with me?" he asked stupidly, so full of himself. He was just that clueless.

Not only was she not into him sexually, but some strange phenomenon that she couldn't even see, had managed to take her whole life.

"Uh!" she blurted out, feeling hot, but her pussy was feeling so good. "Oh yesssss!" she howled, her body exploding, going into a frenzy.

"Awww, daddy did good," he said as he busily whistled while in the shower. He had no clue her praises had everything to do with Getty's invisible presence and nothing to do with him.

"Mmmm, yes. Soooo good," she replied, her body almost lifting off the bed before she collapsed.

She was a slave to Getty, someone she'd never met, yet didn't want to forget. Neither would Getty as he swallowed her essence, coating his tongue as it went down his throat. He'd been so busy chastising Diesel, but he now he'd thrown that all out the window. All it took was one look at Zara, and he forgot he didn't fuck with humans like that.

He was very much used to just fucking them with his massive dick, but with her, he was perfectly fine partaking of her sweet, sweet nectar. Her scent was inside of him and all over his nose, mouth, and chin, running down his neck. Too bad he was invisible. He was enjoying the confused view he'd like to call his new pussy playground.

Then he caught himself. *What the fuck have I done? I gotta go.*

In an instant, he was gone, wiping any memory of his intrusion inside of her hot, slick pussy from her brain. She sat up and looked around as the air quickly resumed to its normal temperature.

"Damn, Hugh," she huffed in confusion as her wetness covered her inner thighs and the sheets underneath her ass. "I need you to that again more often when I doze off."

❧

"You did what?" Diesel growled, mean mugging Getty. "That's sick as fuck, G. Real sick. Even for your ass."

Getty smiled and shrugged, masking how he really

felt. Zara had gotten to him, and he was embarrassed. Unlike Rose, at least she and Diesel had met. With Zara, she had no clue their paths even crossed. He took a peek into Rose's cell and found the name "Bestie". A quick look at her pictures in there made Getty lose all common sense as he dug, even more, getting her name and address.

"Listen, she was asking for it. I could hear it in her thoughts. The girl was more than ready for that. I had to fix it. Ain't that what we do, Diesel? Fix humans?" he asked, waiting for the debate he was hoping occurred. He had to get that heat off of him, so he figured why not take a jab at his best friend.

"Not the same at all, and you fucking know it," Diesel disputed as Getty referred to Rose. "She was in trouble, *real trouble*. What you did was intrusive, a bitch move. Real intrusive and most definitely inappropriate as hell."

"So you going to this Rose's house unannounced, inserting your presence in her life when her father is a mechanic ain't intrusive? D, get the fuck out of here, man," Getty replied, waving him off. "I'm telling you, she wanted it, and it's over now. She doesn't even know it happened."

"But it did!"

Before Diesel's rant went way left, Getty snatched him, landing them both in Diesel's parents' kitchen back in Etan.

"Well, good morning, boys. Hungry?" Diesel's mother asked, her lips pursed as she could tell they were bickering. "And I don't want to be involved, Getty." She gave him a look, rolling her eyes. Usually, whenever they showed up like that, he was the culprit.

"Good morning, Mrs. Weber. You are looking beautiful as ever. And only a crazy man would turn down your good cooking," he smoothly replied, kissing her on the cheek.

Getty had been flirting with her since he was old enough to talk. Before, it was with his eyes, batting, and winking until he could form words. Those words morphed into flirtatious responses the bolder he became about how pretty she was.

Early on, they all knew he would be an Etan whore, but he was still charming and respectful to his elders, nonetheless. As an adult, his compliments were purely innocent since he saw her as a mother figure, yet he was still very overt in his delivery whenever he was around her.

"This boy," she said and giggled, still tickled when he spoke to her like that.

"And you know your son. All he eats is berries and oatmeal or seaweed juices." He wanted to say pussy, too, but he ate pussy even more and would choose it over a real meal.

"As he should," she reminded him, knowing the lifestyle Getty lived.

If he wasn't in the studio making music, he was in the club turning up, eating fried chicken wings and fries.

"They are very good for you and keep you regular."

"Well, every now and again, it's good to have some fish," he said, slipping it in as he grinned at Diesel, who was about to go in on his ass.

"I told you I don't want to know, and I don't care," she said, moving around as she prepared breakfast for her husband. "If you two are really staying, go wash up and have a seat. The wala is warm. Grab a cup," she said, referring to their version of coffee. She took off to check on her husband before either could respond.

"Do that shit again, and I won't play nice, G. Like you are seriously going overboard with this. Her best friend? How did you get her information again?"

Getty snickered, dismissing him as he chose not to answer. He never mentioned how he actually got it earlier, hoping it would slip right on by him. He already knew Diesel would fucking lose it, but it was a test. A test he had now failed miserably, choosing to not confess the part he knew would get sticky. It was also why he waited to do it while they were there at Diesel's parents' house should it come up.

"I, uh, sort of snuck in Rose's spot last night. I went through her cell, her little journal, too." He stopped and smiled, waiting for Diesel's reaction before he went on which was steady yet brewing. "And man," he said and stopped, plopping down on the sofa.

As he closed his eyes and smiled, Diesel felt his body rumbling, close to punching Getty's chest in and ripping out his heart. He hadn't gone through her journal even though he wanted to but figured that was off limits, so he stopped. Besides, the address fed his curiosity and he was full—full of Zara.

"Anyway, I scrolled through her social media and let me tell you—"

Diesel immediately lifted him up, grabbing him by his shirt. He had no clue if she slept nude or what Getty saw, but he didn't like that shit at all. Getty chuckled, watching him fall into his trap but hoped to the Etan elders Diesel wouldn't kill him.

"Don't, because you know I should fucking kill you," he hissed, his voice laced with venom as he gripped him by the throat, lifting him off the floor.

"You're tripping, just like I thought, D," he managed to get out, coughing before Diesel tossed him against the wall, watching as he fell. "Yo, D," he said and coughed, sitting up as he took deep breaths. He was prepared to sing Diesel to sleep with a deadly lullaby, but he took that L since he was wrong. "I let you do that shit because I get it. That's your new toy," he slid in, wiping his lip that started to bleed.

"Bitch ass," Diesel fussed, his chest heaving as he stood over him. "And fuck your lip."

Rose could never be a toy to him. Toys you could put down and move on to something else. Since he couldn't do that with her, she had to be more. He couldn't get through a few minutes of the day without thinking about her, fighting hard not to feel her energy, be all up in her space. Watching him struggle, spiraling out of control made Getty feel bad. He got it. Diesel wasn't like him. He wanted to feel love, be in love, too.

"I'm telling you she's trouble, and you know why I'm tripping, Diesel."

"She's not her," he said, shutting Getty down. "And it's me that's the one who's trouble," he growled lowly, wishing he could calm himself down.

He was in trouble, but he didn't want to be warned. He wanted to be irresponsible for once since the last time wasn't intentional. Besides, it happened so long ago, he figured he had learned since Delilah. He was wiser and older now, stronger too...or so he thought.

Getty realized now just how serious it was that he overstepped, quickly finding a way to defuse it. He needed more time to get to his friend, but this way wasn't it. Not if it sent Diesel to a dark place, a place he couldn't get to him. He was already creating a shield, putting up a guard, blocking him out. So he had to find another way or risk losing his best friend.

"Look," he said and sighed, wiping his lip. "She was fully clothed, I swear. And I didn't go through her journal or social media. Just her cell. I did see it though. And for the record, she was wrapped up like a mummy. D, I wouldn't lie to you. Besides, you will fucking listen in on my thoughts at some point if I did. I swear, man. You gotta chill," he begged him, holding both hands up in surrender. "I was there for five minutes, maybe. And I went with very good intentions."

"And in five minutes, you got her girl's information and didn't even try to disrobe her? See some pussy? Yeah, right."

"See, it's that right there! That response is why I needed to know how she got down. If Rose is anything like Zara, I can feel the trouble *we* will be in."

"Why is this a 'we' thing, Getty?" he asked in a forced whisper. "You know what? Never mind, I get it. I'm weak, weak as fuck. Oh, and I am undeserving of a fucking relationship. I'm not Getty, the pussy hunter and tamer. I need you to save me from myself," he said in a whiny way, mimicking a female in a facetious manner. "Thanks for the concern, but I'm out. Tell my mom when she comes down while you're eye fucking her," he said, vanishing quickly as he returned to his apartment.

I'm sorry, D. I just can't lose you, Getty said to him. *You're more than a friend. You're my brother. And I can't help your mom has a fat ass. And a pretty ass smile.*

Diesel was furious, yet he couldn't help but laugh after hearing that. He knew Getty meant no harm, but if his father heard that, there was no coming back. Getty would be a dead ass Etan after flirting with his wife.

Well, act like it then, bitch. Be my brother, my best friend.

I am, D.

Then, this time, trust me or at least let me live a little, G. Delilah was handled.

And it almost killed me... and you. Just be careful, Diesel.

Yeah, give my mom a kiss for me. Tell her that I love her. We'll rap later. Fuck with me then.

Getty nodded in lieu of responding. All he could think about was Delilah and how she fucked up Diesel's life with her perfectly, human self. She and Getty had met in 1930 in Atlanta. He was a musician at the Metropolitan Opera House, where she also played.

Diesel, being the one to always support him, would show up at each performance. The crowds came in droves to hear Getty, but the one who stole the show off of her pure beauty was Delilah. Like fire, Diesel became consumed with her, showing up night after night as she played her violin. It was intoxicating and empowering in the way she got him to confess who he really was.

"Leave him be," Getty heard Diesel's mother say. She heard most of what they'd argued about, wishing it weren't true. Even though she was human, it took a lot for her and Darian, Diesel's father, to get the elders' blessing once Darian had fallen in love with her. It wasn't intentional, but if the Etans really knew why he had to have his wife, Ann, she'd be crowned the head of Etan. She saved his existence. She saved him.

"Mrs. Weber, you know your son," he said and laughed. "It was just me teasing."

She gave him a look, lifting her brow. She'd become more like the Etans than she cared to admit. While she didn't possess their powers, she was granted one chance to drink from a fountain that transformed her human body, making her practically immortal.

"All women are not like her. At least give him a little room to figure it out for himself. Besides, that was long ago. You know my precious Darian," she said, calling Diesel by his real name. "The moment we say no or he can't, that's when he will or fight like hell trying. I can't lose my son, Getty. Please don't push him. Just watch him, watch him quietly. Be there for him, and when he really is in trouble, you let us know. Understand?"

"Yes, ma'am," was all he said, knowing he was on to something.

"Getty?" she said, warning him.

"I will, I promise."

"Just don't jump the gun, and stop letting him know you're watching and listening in. A man's thoughts about a woman are sacred if he really cares about her. Give him some space to be normal, human even. Isn't that why you two have chosen to be on Earth?"

"That, and well..."

"Getty Moore, do you want me to call your mother? Sharon would not be happy."

"Shoot, my mama knows what's up with her baby boy." He grinned, walking up and hugging her. "Y'all both know me and love me," he said, kissing her on the cheek.

"Watch it."

"Hey, a man's old habits are sometimes hard to break."

"Ahhh, but they are breakable. You should try breaking a few of your own."

Getty laughed at that. He had no habits he wanted to part with. Not one at all.

"And remember, he's human."

"Not fully," he reminded her. "And he hates being reminded of that, Mrs. Weber. You know that."

"I do, but one day, he will see that with the right one and at the right time, being who he is, both human and Etan, is a gift."

Getty smiled. He loved him some Mrs. Weber. Especially her motherly, protective instinct. It was so sexy to him. She was indeed a beauty, one of a dark hue that was close to Rose's complexion. When he caught himself flirting and possibly thinking out loud, he heard Mr. Weber moving around upstairs and decided it was time to go.

Shit, I do need help. And more of Zara. Sweet pussy, Zara.

"I'm about to get up out of here, but I have one question," he asked, hoping he got an answer he could live with, one that would make him try to see life through Diesel's eyes.

"How did you know that D's father was for you?"

"If I tell you, I may have to hurt you myself," she replied with a wink of the eye. "But I will say this. It was the absolute best decision *for me*. I gave up my life, my existence, to become one of you, I suppose, and I wouldn't change a thing. Imagine if my family chose for me, Getty? Just imagine."

He heard her loud and clear, thinking about Zara. A smile appeared, but he wiped it off immediately. Mrs. Weber caught it but said nothing. Whatever it was he was thinking, she'd hoped it worked in all of their favor.

"Just know that when it's pure love, a selfless love, it has no limitations, no boundaries. It is what it is. Let him find it, and maybe one day, you'll find yours. I know my Diesel. He's brilliant but always struggled with not being enough. To some, he wasn't human enough. To others, he wasn't Etan enough. Maybe, just maybe, his love is there... on Earth."

"Naw, I don't buy it," Getty said, not feeling that at all. He knew how irresponsible and unpredictable humans could be. He wasn't letting his best friend go that far, but he would do as she said.

"It's not your journey, Getty. It's his. Just do as I say,

please and thank you," she said, lowering her voice as her husband could be heard coming downstairs.

"Just know he's going hard with these humans, and this one is cute," Getty said, then looked around quickly to see if Diesel popped back up. He never knew with that one.

"Oh, be careful. He might get you when you get back. I see the lip," she said and giggled. "I love you, Getty."

Before he could say that he loved her too, they heard, "Ann, you tell Getty that when I get down there, I'm whooping his ass! You're my wife. He needs to get his own, damn it!"

6

"If you can't come, Rose, then I will have to give away your job," her boss, Roscoe, told her. He was already old and now irritated to hear he was losing his best waitress.

"But it's just a week, Mr. Roscoe. I will do anything when I get back to make it up to you. I will come in an hour or two early or stay late. Who needs sleep?" she scoffed, waving her hand in the air. She was desperate. One check short, and she would be facing eviction. "Please don't. I need this job," she pleaded. She managed to catch an Uber over there after Diesel left, wanting to talk to her boss face-to-face, but it wasn't working out so well.

Mr. Roscoe hated being so harsh and direct, but once he replaced her, he knew the chances of hiring her again were slim. His diner did well, but it was old and needed quite a bit of renovation. He needed help, but not enough to hire one extra person once her job was filled.

"Look, I have to put out a help wanted sign. If no one applies within a week or the person doesn't work out before you come back, the job is yours. But I can't promise you a job in a week's time. I'm sorry, Rose. It's busy," he said, wiping the counter down to avoid looking at her.

He was a grouchy old man, but he had a soft spot for her. Still, his soft spot wouldn't pay the diner's overheard and keep money coming in being slow.

While she could hear the sincerity in his voice, she felt doomed. She never was the begging kind, so her begging had already taken its toll.

"Fine," she said quietly, giving up. "I get it. And thanks." As she struggled to make it out of the front door, he came around to help her. After squeezing her lightly on the shoulder, Rose nodded as she carefully made her way to the Uber. It cost her a few more bucks than a bus, but she needed her crutches to fit in easily as she rode, so an Uber it was.

She stopped to catch a tear, hurrying along before she had a meltdown. She could always stay with her father to cut back on expenses or even get a temp job, but a temp job could be anywhere in terms of location. The diner, just like her apartment, was relatively close to stores for groceries and buses to get to school.

As the Uber pulled off with a teary-eyed Rose inside, Diesel sat across the street fuming. He wasn't sure why she couldn't catch a break. He also knew his presence would only complicate her life, but he couldn't let go.

Even watching her struggle to get in the Uber, took everything in him to restrain himself and not interfere. Once she did, he went inside the diner.

He stood at the door, watching the two old waitresses manage the diner while Roscoe was in the back fussing at the cook. The place wasn't much to look at, but he could tell the food was good as it was packed to capacity.

"Dining in or takeout?" the old waitress with the name tag Alice asked him. She was chewing gum like her jaws hurt, her mouth long and wide like a cow.

"Dining in. The counter is fine," he said as he watched her grab a menu.

Her hair was a silvery blue from years of coloring it, and her uniform looked like it'd seen better days. Still, the food smelled good, and the customers sat around either eating or eagerly waiting for their meal.

"Lunch special just started," she said, pointing to the section on the back. "Remember, it's pork chop Wednesday."

Diesel frowned, thinking about the pork cooked in lard. His stomach churned as she walked away, looking at anything on the menu that resembled something edible.

"Thank you for coming to Roscoe's Dine, Wine, and Swine. How can I help you?" It was Roscoe, looking past him as the two women moved about taking orders. He knew they couldn't handle the night shift too. His mouth twitched as he prepared himself to post a help wanted sign.

"You can help me by allowing Rose Steel to work the register behind this counter. She can also help prep meals that allow her to sit down when she comes on and start the dishwasher. Even help dry them if she can sit while doing it. Nod if you understand," Diesel instructed him, looking him directly in the eye. His voice was normal, but it had a stern, hypnotizing tone that reeled Roscoe in.

Roscoe nodded his head.

Diesel asked him, "Now, when Rose calls you back, because she will, what will you tell her?"

"That she can work the register, prep meals, and ummm, uh, uh—"

Diesel leaned his head down, his steel-like eyes boring deeply into Roscoe's, who immediately smiled. "And help with washing and drying dishes."

"Very good. Now, may I have an order shrimp and grits to go? The way Rose likes them. That will be all."

"You got it," Roscoe told him, taking off as he whistled.

Diesel sighed, promising himself this was the last time he would intrude in her life. He looked at his watch, realizing he needed to get to the shop to fix her car. He had a small, steady crew of mechanics, but he'd kill someone if it broke down again. So he decided it would be him to fix it.

"She's going to fuss," he said and laughed, thinking about her reaction when he showed up, once again, with food.

He could tell from Rose's thin frame that she either barely ate or had a fast metabolism. Either way, she needed to eat, especially if she was taking pain medication.

"Here you go. A nice helping of our good ole shrimp and grits! The best in town. Yessiree, buddy," Roscoe said in a chipper manner.

Diesel shook his head, looking at the effects of the simple cast he spelled. Roscoe was acting way too strange, but it was his fault. He knew he laid it on him way too strong and hoped it wore off in the minutes after he left.

"And thanks. I'm sure Rose is going to love them," he replied with a slim grin on his face, revealing his teeth. Roscoe smiled back in amazement, nodding in his head as if he'd never seen gold, diamond teeth before. "Have a great one."

"I'm coming over," Zara told Rose, grabbing her book bag off of the floor.

"Zara, no. I'm fine," she insisted, wincing from pain.

"You are such an awful liar, Rosey."

"You know I hate that name," Rose fussed. She had been looking at a blank screen on television since she got back from the diner.

"Well, you know I hate when you act like you don't need anything or anyone. I'm your best friend."

"Exactly. My best friend, not my parent. I did not break my foot, Zara. Just bruised it. There's a little swelling. That's all."

"Which you still won't tell me how it happened," she said, walking to the cafeteria to grab a cup of coffee. "I'm used to you being here so we can chat over coffee, and you're being so stubborn. I still can't believe you didn't call me last night. I keep telling you I can let you drive my truck. I barely use it, and it's only a year old. Shoot, you can have it." Zara owned a Range Rover, but to her, it was just a truck. It meant nothing to her, especially when her best friend had a piece-of-shit car.

"It was late and raining. Plus, I didn't want to hear Hugh's mouth, and no, thank you. My Mustang is just fine. She just needs a little work."

"You mean a lot of work, but I digress. And Hugh adores you, Rose. Why would he have a problem with me helping you? It was a gift to me, so it's mine to use or not use as I see fit."

"A gift for what?" Rose mumbled, almost knowing the answer.

"Whatever, girl," she said, laughing. "I can't help that he's enthralled with my rather-amazing sexual skills."

"Oh God, Zara. Stop it," Rose replied, giggling. "That man is going to buy you more than a car a lot sooner. I say ease up just a little."

"No, it's him that needs to pick it up a bit. Maybe buy him something to keep it hard, make that shit blow up big—anything, if you know what I mean."

"Nope! Not going there with you today. And at least you're getting some. All I get are lames hitting on me that sit outside. Can't get to the corner where I live without that happening at least once a day. Besides, it's early, and I want to cry myself to sleep. I just don't know what else could happen now, but I don't want to."

"Nothing else will happen because, so after class, I'm coming over. I got you, Rosey. Hugh's already mad because I didn't make breakfast this morning. Well, not the blueberry muffins. For some reason, his ass loves those blueberry muffins. We ran out of it," she said dismissively, hoping his anger would make him come home and tear up the pussy.

"That man's got to eat, Zara. Really?"

"That's the thing!" she squawked. "I did cook, but

then I remembered we ran out of Jiffy mix. Then..." she said and paused, scratching her head. "I don't even know what happened. By the time he got out, I had just enough time to whip up an omelet. He took off all mad, but whatever. I need a break from him anyway. I swear I feel like I'm in a relationship with my father sometimes."

Rose felt her skin cringe thinking about Hugh. He'd never said or done anything inappropriately, but he was way too friendly for her liking. Their freshman year, he'd set his sights on Zara. Almost ten years her senior, Rose thought it strange he'd never married, given how good looking he was. But his sometimes pompous attitude was a turnoff, too. She honestly felt he didn't like her, although he never indicated that. It was as if he pitied her, and if you knew Rose Steel, pity was a trigger for her.

Zara, after giving in to her parents' desire, painfully pretended to be happy in front of everyone except Rose. With Rose, she could be herself. With Rose, she could say she was scared or be her hypersexual self, but not with her parents, or at least her mother.

She was always at the top of her class from kindergarten through college and anything else she pretty much showed interest in.

She was even on the school's volleyball team, often known for being aggressive while Rose was the quiet, studious one who hung out at the library. When they first met, Zara looked at Rose as competition, often outscoring her on tests, but her strong work ethic and very little need for idle chatter drew Zara in. For once, she saw another female as someone who simply wanted to win, not *be her* or beat her.

"Got dammit!" Zara screeched, her coffee spilling all over her lab coat. "Are you fucking blind?" she yelled as she tried to wipe the excess coffee away that seeped further into her clothing.

"I could be if that means I keep running into you," Getty said, grinning as he took her all in. She looked even more stunning than before.

He licked his lips as he remembered the taste of her pussy in his mouth. His eyes dropped quick, staring at her nipples through her top. He winced, remembering how he twisted and turned them as he consumed them. His member rose without warning, and just that fast, he was ready to fuck her quiet, making her submit to him. And he could, he really could.

"What? You're just going to stand there and gawk at me? Such a fucking asshole," she grumbled, fists balled up. "Hey, weirdo, guess what? You're buying me another cup and paying for my dry cleaning."

Getty smiled, watching her get heated.

"I swear this guy is going to make me late. Just pay me," she demanded lowly, holding her hand out as he stood there annoying her with no response. The angrier she got, the better he felt.

"Zara, who is that?" Rose asked, very concerned. Zara didn't back down from many, and if she did, it was only until she had a plan to get back at them later. She was a scheming something when she wanted to be, sparing Rose of her wrath since they were best friends.

"Some damn freak, girl! All smiling at me. He basically ran into me, knocking my coffee all over me. Probably these damn dark shades he's wearing inside the building," she complained.

As she did, Getty chuckled and crossed his arms. He stood with his legs stretched apart as if he were watching a movie.

"Don't you smile at me! How about you just pay me for my dry cleaning and get me a cup of coffee, *errand boy*," she growled, ready to smack him if he chuckled one more time.

"Zara!" Rose screamed. "I'm coming right now. This is crazy! Just stop it!"

While Rose rambled on, trying to figure out how she could get up and out of there with her crutches, Getty's eyes left Zara's pouty and sexy yet rage-filled mouth and traveled down to her round and fat ass.

Damn, I got to have that. All of that.

"Fool! Do you hear me?"

Fuck no, he said to himself, silencing her and everyone around her. As the room stood still, Getty took a stroll around her one good time.

"I should take you right here," he whispered in her

ear, then sniffed her. "Sweet ass. Now, because you're so fucking fine, when I release you, you're going to give me your number. Hell, and forget you're angry with me. Then I'm going to leave and call you later. Who knows what I will say, but keep this same energy, ma. This same got damn energy," he said. "Now, what's your number?"

As she belted out her number, he memorized it, watching her lips and tongue as she spoke each syllable like it was honey dripping off of a honeycomb.

"What's your full name, sweetness?" he asked, fighting hard not to laugh in her face.

"Zara. Zara Grey. And I'm so sorry. I can't believe I bumped into you." By this time, she'd hung up on Rose.

"What the hell is going on?" Rose asked, looking at the cell. "Ugh," she screamed in frustration, throwing herself on the bed. "This is not my day either. I hate my life."

"Don't forget to call me," she said. "And again, I'm really sorry."

"Forget you? Girl, never. Everything about you is right here," he said, pointing to his temple. "And here," he finished, covering the left side of his chest over his heart.

"Really?" Zara giggled like she swallowed a glass of laughing gas. She had no clue why she was so giddy.

"I like that," he said, his smile dropping as he

wished he produced that response from her naturally on his own.

Getty pulled out his wallet and produced a fifty-dollar bill. He bent down and whispered in her ear, “For your coffee and dry cleaning. And once I walk away, this never happened,” he said, gently rubbing her cheek. He couldn’t do it. He just couldn’t do it. His conscience ate at him after his talk with Mrs. Weber.

Slowly inhaling, Zara looked Getty in the eyes and nodded.

“Trust me, I’m a fucking jerk,” he told her and laughed. “Get that shirt clean. Be good, ma,” he said, quickly taking off.

“Damn it,” she gasped once he was gone, looking down at her shirt. “How did this happened? Oh, God. This is so not my day. I hate my life,” she groaned, ironically sounding just like Rose.

As she stomped off to the bookstore to quickly buy an UM T-shirt, Getty jetted off, disappearing into thin air. But no matter how far away he’d gotten from her, the more he felt her energy, craving her when he landed in his bedroom on his back in the bed.

“I need some pussy,” he said to himself. To some, it was alcohol or drugs, but to Getty, it was always the female anatomy—pussy. “Angelica,” he said, appearing within seconds back in Etan, but this time, ready for some action.

“I’m busy,” Angelica told him with an attitude. She

was lying on her stomach, sunbathing in the Etan sun in her backyard. She was naked, a bronze beauty that all the Etans admired, but only one had her heart —Getty.

One tug of her thick, long mane stretching her neck, and she felt as if she were melting as his tongue tasted her skin, which burned so good… like she was on fire.

"You are never too busy for me," he hissed, sliding his thick fingers down the crack of her ass until they landed between the lips of her vagina. "See, even *she* knows."

One slip of his finger inside of her caused Angelica to have a full body orgasm.

"I—I'm tired, Getty. Tired of playing this game." She could barely speak as he transformed her backyard into his dungeon that was filled with every sex toy imaginable. As he pulled her and wrapped her wrists behind her back, Angelica became one with him.

She could stop him if she wanted to, but when they were in the dungeon, he was always in control. Hell, if she were being honest, he was *always* in control, no matter where they were. The only rules that counted were Getty, and she was to blame for that. She'd broken him, and she would forever pay for that.

No one told her they'd be going through this for years, but she'd brought it upon herself. She made a stupid bet with her fellow Moons that she'd get Getty and not only in bed but in his heart. He was the asshole of all assholes but imagine to her surprise when he was anything but that once she'd gotten to know him.

All the Moon girls were waiting for her to break up with him, pay him back for all the hearts he'd broken, but she couldn't do it. She just couldn't, but she did once her secret was revealed. Being a Solar meant he could be at any place at any time. Angelica let her guard down one day, laughing at him behind his back.

She didn't mean a word of it as he sat by listening while she'd made a fool of him. The Solar and Moon factions had a love-hate relationship. Other than the fairies who were mostly sought out for wisdom and guidance, the Solars and Moons were free to live their lives for the greater good of Etan.

That was hundreds of years ago, and Getty refused to forgive her, but he couldn't deny that she was the best fuck of all fucks. And she was beautiful and lethal. It was her love for him, however, that wouldn't allow her gifts to harm him.

She was the great Angelina, the quiet assassinator, the silent weapon of war. And whenever danger neared, she could convert herself into any animal—a snake being her go-to, as it was easy to hide and enter places without being seen. One bite, and your entire being turn into a pile of useless glob instantly.

"Uh, you're hurting me," she said, wincing as he pulled her up.

"Stand," he demanded, kicking one leg out so her

legs were stretched apart as she stood. He grabbed a satin blindfold, lifting her hair as he tied it over her eyes. Her bronze breasts sat up firmly, going up and down as she breathed in anticipation of his entry.

Getty was not only a beautiful, warm brown-colored Etan. He was a well-endowed one, stretching her entry as far as the east was from the west. If he happened to string a tune while in the midst of a stroke, the orgasms he created would make a woman literally go insane.

"Getty," she whimpered, feeling her body about to shift.

"You better fucking not. Don't play with me," he growled, forcing her to take it as he began to hum. "Always wanting to do some shit to prove you can."

"I—I'm not. I, mmmm," she moaned lowly as he issued long and deep strokes, bringing her under his submission.

"Yeah, that's it," he managed to say, their bodies rapidly shaking as their energies created an overwhelming high that could kill a human. "Take this dick."

From him pulling her by her arms, she stood with her back against his stomach with him inside of her.

"If you ever try to manipulate me again, I will hurt you, and you know how."

She did. Hurting her was him cutting her completely off, banishing her presence from his life. The last time he did, she almost died of depression, abandoning her passion and power until he returned to her. Her family and practically all of the Moons despised the hold Getty had on her and they weren't even a couple. Far from one, but tell that to Angelica's heart.

Unlike the Solars, her faction couldn't survive on Earth for long periods of time. No, the Moons couldn't endure the environmental stressors of being on Earth. The exposure to the sun too long killed them.

During the times he stalled her when he wasn't on Earth, he'd find pleasure in another woman from the Moon faction. Her name was Leeta. Leeta, deathly afraid of Angelica, wouldn't even go near him now, killing any friendship or sexual relations they could've had. Yet Getty tried every chance he could to break Angelica down. He did, over and over.

"No, no, no! Please don't!" she yelled as he wound his hips deep inside of her, the tip of his dick touching her cervix. "Oh, fuck!"

"Yes, and any out of control shit from you once I leave, and I'm good on you, Angelica," he hissed, sinking his teeth on her shoulder. "I fuck who I want, when I want to."

"But you promised me," she cried out as he played in her pussy, making her come again.

"And you promised me, too, and you lied again," he said, thinking of her on-again, off-again boyfriend. The dungeon was the only place he'd entertain her, refusing to be seen publicly with her.

"I won't. Just don't leave me again," she cried, her slickness running down her thighs against his balls.

Sadly, Getty's mind was already back on Earth. He rammed her even harder as he tried to block Zara out.

"Don't," he warned her, watching her as she tried to give him eye contact.

"Please," she begged, wishing he'd just give in to her. "Getty, baby. Please.

"Fuck no. Shut the fuck up," he grunted, pushing her down roughly as he released on her backside. "Just don't say shit."

Without any warning, she was back in her backyard alone, and he was gone. He couldn't bear to look at her for too long and not get angry.

"Fucking humans. What is it about you?" he hissed as he watched Zara leaving class, landing right back to where she was. Even after he'd just hit Angelica.

He liked the subtle naughty look she had when she wore her lab coat and scrub top, but that tight ass UM T-shirt made him want to devour her. He was so worried about Diesel and Rose, he missed it was him that was in denial, needing someone to watch after him. He was moving just as reckless, if not more.

7

"Just knock on the door and leave it," Diesel whispered to himself. He knew the grits would be cold soon, but his nerves were out of control. *Imagine that. Me scared of a woman.*

To most of the women he came across throughout his usual routine, he was untouchable, even dismissive. He was polite but short. Sometimes he gave them an Earth-shattering yet lazy smile. Others he'd even flirt with, most times making their day, but intimacy was off-limits. It was either a few words or straight to fucking. And those he'd fuck knew it was just that. He didn't dive into casual sex. Repeats led to confusion, like cuddling, laying up, and sharing, too.

Sharing was way too intimate for him. It was a place that got him in trouble. Delilah was proof of that. He grimaced thinking of Delilah, yet one thought of Rose, and his common sense wasn't common anymore. Now, here he was, again, feelings rushing and overflowing... for Rose. He was a goner, and he hadn't even touched her yet, tasted her either.

Fucking lunatic, he hissed to himself. If he could, he'd handle Delilah yet again, hating she still stirred up such emotions.

Even the look he hid behind was a mask. He was beyond gorgeous. His sex appeal natural, but the thugged-out, menacing approach was nothing but a means to getting easy pussy when he wanted it and, more importantly, to guard his heart.

Who the hell am I fooling? he thought and laughed. His guard was down, and she did that to him. Rose did that and more. He grunted, thinking of Rose and her sweet-smelling pussy. It smelled of apples, warm apples, like apple pie. He stood there, going through a mental tug-of-war of denial versus giving in while a few other people that lived on her floor stared at him confused, wondering if he was high or a serial rapist.

He laughed, hearing their thoughts when a few of them had their own demons, mostly ones he had no qualms about, but one thought that spoke of Rose, and that person may not have made it past him, let alone out her apartment building.

While he stood there for what seemed forever outside her door, Rose sat around on her bed, thinking of what was in the refrigerator to eat. Grocery shopping was a necessity yet something she didn't do that often for two reasons—lack of time and definitely very little money.

Her diet consisted of whatever she found in the school's cafe, got from the diner, or got from Sunday dinner at her daddy's house. Sure, she moseyed into a nearby spot to eat when she found a spare hour or two in between studying over a long weekend, but now she was stuck, looking at her foot.

"Gosh, I'm so freaking hungry and clumsy," Rose said to herself.

She couldn't wait for Zara to come over, knowing she might be able to get Zara's greedy behind to bring her something to eat. If nothing else, Zara loved to eat. Her thickness was proof of it, although she had a washboard stomach, compliments of the personal gym she and Hugh had in their home.

"Naw, that's selfish," she mumbled, sitting up on her elbows in the middle of her bed. "Let me see what I got in here."

After scooting out of bed and reaching for her crutches, Rose took her time stabilizing them as she pushed up and stood.

"Whew," she said, then swung her way unsteadily to the kitchen. Rose was naturally clumsy, and adding crutches didn't quite help. Once she did make it without incident, she took a deep breath and opened her refrigerator. "Damn," she groaned, seeing the fruits of her labor or the lack thereof if she was honest. It was a sign that she was a poor, very poor college student and a very hungry one as her stomach rumbled.

She didn't have to peek, glaring at the half carton of eggs, some jerk turkey lunch meat, yogurt, and half cup of tomato soup from the diner.

"I guess it's you and me, baby," she said, grabbing the key lime yogurt. She held it, leaning against the counter.

She tried opening it up but struggled as the aluminum foil jammed up on her. By the time the foil gave some, the yogurt flew up in the air, then hit the floor.

"Oh my God!" she fussed, looking at the yogurt splattered all across her floor. She wanted to cry, not hearing the door that rattled when knocked on. As the knocks grew louder, she quickly turned her head and smiled. "Yes, must be Zara," she said. "Guess she decided to ditch class after arguing with the crazy guy."

As she made her way over, she froze when she heard him shout, "Rose! Rose! Open up!"

"What the hell?" she fussed. Taking slow steps and swings, she made it to the door and opened it and wasn't too happy. "Diesel?"

"Shit," he mumbled, gulping at her beauty. "I mean —Hey, Rose." He didn't mean to curse, but that was a minor offense compared to what he was thinking.

Baby girl spared nothing, wearing a pair of black

tights and a thinly strapped, yellow tank top. Her hair was a mass of curls, almost bigger than her. He knew she had hair but it was all wild, being left to do what it wanted freely. It made him want to rush her and her hair, taming them both.

"What happened now?" she asked, still not moving to let him in.

In almost forty-eight hours, they were practically inseparable. She wasn't that friendly, and their paths crossing had been a result of her mishaps. She was starting to think one of them had a lifetime date with bad luck.

Then it hit her. "Dang, the car can't be fixed, huh?"

"What? Oh, hell naw," he quickly said, recovering as he shook his head and stretched his eyes.

And like always, she smelled delightful, this time a mixture of berries folded into apples.

I love fucking berries. Focus, D. Fucking focus.

"The car will be fixed in a day or so. I was hungry after our trip to the ER and grabbed me something to eat. Figured you needed something to eat too, and oh, these," he said, holding up her medicine. "You forgot them."

Rose sighed, closing her eyes. She stepped back just a little, holding the door to let him in. "I bet you think I am such a clumsy, forgetful idiot," she said, as he stepped in and turned around.

Not at all. You are so beautiful, Rose. Fucking beautiful.

"No, not even. Remember, it was me that sort of caused your foot to be hurt," he said quickly, refusing to say what he really felt about her.

Too soon. Way too soon, Diesel, he told himself.

"Hmmm, I guess," she said, then remembered he stopped to help her after her car broke down, so she reasoned they were even.

"Oh, where do you want me to put this? It's shrimp and grits. Heard it's a favorite by many at the diner."

She smiled. "Well, it is. How did you know that? Matter a fact, I don't think I've never seen you there. It's where I work," she revealed, looking at him skeptically as she closed the door. "Sorry," she said, adjusting the crutches under her arms. "You know me..." she said and laughed. "The clumsy one."

"Don't apologize. And I came unannounced, but your ass is clumsy," he slid in as he took a deep breath and exhaled.

The air itself was high in her presence, making him feel like he was on top of two worlds.

"Now you can't keep coming by unannounced, then insulting me," she teased him, lifting her brow.

"I know. I'm impulsive at times. Bad habit, and I'd take being around your clumsy self any day," he said, hoping that bought him some grace. He looked quickly down the hall where he knew she slept, jaw tightening when he thought of Getty being in there.

"So... the food?" she said, wondering when he was

going to release it and let her dig in it. She was tiny, but Rose could eat.

"I asked where you wanted me to put it." He laughed, placing it on the coffee table as he approached her. "Here, let me help. You look like you're tired."

She was, and he felt it, but he also felt something else—a rush of excitement as he drew near her. He learned to move slow around humans. Etans' natural rhythm was naturally fast as a means of survival but really because an Etan's life moved faster in general.

As he slowly took one crutch, she gripped him tightly.

"Easy, Rose. I got you," he told her, grabbing the other.

Then in one swoop, she was in his arms. She grew warm, licking her lips as he mentally licked them back.

Easy, D. Go easy.

"You have to stop doing this," she whispered, studying every detail of his face, mostly his thick eyebrows and down to his lazy, brown eyes. His lips were full and kissable, his teeth she'd grown to love with the edge of hoodness to them as he grinned. And when he did, Rose swore her pussy jumped.

"What? Feeding you?"

Yup, food and more, she thought, causing him to laugh when he heard that.

To recover, he quickly sat her in the chair near the coffee table with the speed of lightning. If she thought that one more time, he was close to having his way with her and asking for forgiveness later.

Unsure of what to do next, he rubbed his hands against his jeans—jeans she'd rather see off his body that hung low on his waist. His swag had Rose all in, forgetting she was hungry or had a hurt foot as he stood there, sweating profusely, blocking her thoughts out.

"How do you do that?" she asked, suddenly realizing she was sitting back in the chair so fast.

"What?" He feigned confusion.

"That, that thing you just did that got me here," she said, suspicion settling in again.

"You tripping, Rose," he said, dismissing as he sniffed around.

If Getty had been back, this house visit was getting cut short. Giving his attention back to her, he grinned the same goofy way she was. They were babbling silent like fools in their heads about how they felt or thought until he spoke.

"So uh, you need food and then these," he said, pulling her meds out of his back pocket.

"If you say so. Hey, can you bring me my hand sanitizer? I would have washed my hands, but your Superman ass came in here in took over," she teased him, laughing.

"Is that right? You're into superheroes? You like Superman?"

"Oh boy, do I?" she gushed. It was a common love she and her father shared.

She remembered Saturday mornings after her mother died. Her father had no clue how to raise a girl, so they watched cartoons, and as a treat, they go downtown to the comic bookstore.

"And my favorite isn't Superman," she quipped, then rolled her eyes.

"Who is it then? The Black Panther?"

Diesel loved that movie. It held many secrets he found similar to Etan, the one that exposed who his father really was to his mother.

"What is that boy out there doing now?" Darian asked, watching his wife bite her nails as she looked through the window.

She was always worried about their only child, but he had no clue why.

He was nicknamed Diesel for reasons more than he shared. His son was tough, tougher than most kids, making him a proud father. He'd watch Diesel fall and get a scrape or bruise that barely lasted a day if that. His mother, Ann, would lose it, then watch it practically disappear, healing quickly. She even asked the doctors during routine visits, but most wrote her inquiries off as being an overly concerned mother, especially a first-time mother.

"He's helping a boy. It's so strange. It's like he couldn't even stand at first, but now he is and almost as if nothing happened," she said, turning around to stare at her husband.

Darian was gorgeous, a dark-chocolate treat each time she saw him. Their son was the spitting image of his father, short of being a tad lighter because of her lightly tanned complexion.

"He's at it again, huh? My boy is something else," he said nervously, wrapping his arms around her as he went in for a kiss. He was such a good lover.

She wondered why she hadn't gotten pregnant yet again. It had been almost five years, and Diesel was sprouting up to be big and strong.

"Ann, relax. Why do you fuss so much over him? That's what he does. He likes helping people."

As he kissed her on the forehead, she closed her eyes and welcomed the hold he had on her. Darian was big himself, so big she felt like a little child being cradled in his arms as he bear-hugged her.

"But it's more," she whispered into his chest. "I even notice it when he touches me or when I'm sad. It's like he knows and is coming to my rescue. And if I am feeling bad, by the time he goes away, I somehow feel better. I—I don't know. Maybe it's—"

"Ann, baby, I need to tell you something."

And when his father did, the love he had for Ann couldn't compare to the love she had for him. On the run for a while back then, although with his best friend, Ezrah, together they all faced their elders, returning to their world of Etan.

Diesel was confused, leaving their life on Earth

behind, but once he became a man, he had the chance to return, and he did. Now he felt he knew the reason —Rose.

"And no, it's not The Black Panther," she told him quickly, laughing. "You're so silly. It's actually Batman, if you must know."

"Batman?"

"Yeah, and go get my sanitizer so I can eat," she told him, pushing his thigh.

"Did I ever tell you that you're a little bossy?"

"A few times, and this is coming from the man who keeps popping up in my personal space. You shouldn't talk. Now go. It's in my bathroom down the hall."

"Whatever," he grumbled, turning around to do as she said, but smiled when she couldn't seem him. He could get used to this.

"And Diesel?" she called out, and he stopped, dropping the smile when he turned around.

"You changed your mind, huh? Want me to carry you to the bathroom, too?" he said, trying to be funny. Oh, he wished she really did, and he would do it, too, hearing her thoughts that seemed to not think it was a bad idea.

"No, I just wanted to say thank you... for barging into my life. See? I was raised properly," she said, low key being shady but in a complimentary way.

"Yeah, properly but still bossy. Sit tight, clumsy girl," he shot back at her.

As he walked off, Rose sat back and stared. Immediately, just like him, she too thought she could get used to having him around, even if he was forcing her to actually break up her routine and do something different. School required a lot of discipline, but even most of the other students came back to class from over the weekend, talking about how they caught a movie, went to the mall, or hung out with friends.

Hers wasn't exactly a money thing. She could always find something cheap to do. She just didn't do a lot of people, and Zara was more than enough.

"Relax, D. You can do this. Just make sure she takes her meds and eat and then get this car back here," he said, looking in the mirror as he washed his hands, tossing some water on his face.

He closed his eyes, wishing he could be normal for once. He felt her energy, and it was driving him insane. After washing his hands, he grabbed a few paper towels and dried them off, then did something he knew he shouldn't have done—he immobilized her. Stopping her mid sentence from saying something as he walked around her room, spying.

"Of course, she's a fucking neat freak. A med head," he said and laughed, shaking his head.

Her place was small but definitely clean and girly. While complete with a simple bedroom set, Rose still managed to consume her bed with a massive amount of pillows, enough for three people. He saw her small slippers nearby and a footstool he assumed was used to reach for things up high in her closet or even to climb on her bed, given her height without shoes.

He opened her nightstand and found the journal, tapping it. He so badly wanted to pull back the pages and read her intimate thoughts. The ones he heard made him feel chaotic and unstable, even the happy which didn't happen that often in his day to day life. But her journal, he could dive in and really dissect what the fuck was really up with Rose Steel.

"Naw, that's some fuck boy shit," he reasoned with himself, thinking of Getty. He wanted the girl, but if he got her, it wouldn't be like this. Besides, he was enjoying this dance, this tempo of cat and mouse they started. Diesel closed the drawer quickly and walked out of her room.

"Oh, the hand sanitizer," he said, reaching in the bathroom and grabbing it. Once he was out of the bathroom, he released her. "Sorry," he said, walking toward her as she ogled him like he was a piece a meat. *Got damn it. She better stop that shit.*

"Hurry. I'm hungry." She laughed, reaching for it. "You mind doing one more thing?"

"And she knows how to ask questions instead of barking orders."

"Yeah, yeah," she said, pumping the pump a few times before she rigorously cleaned her hands.

Wincing, Diesel wondered if she would work them

as good on his dick. She looked up and smiled innocently.

"I have a bottle of Welch's grape juice in the cabinet. You mind getting it and pouring me a glass? Ice is in the freezer."

"Not at all. Anything else, your highness?"

"Boy, don't start that crap. Look around, I'm poor." She laughed. "I'm surprised I got that in there. Just remembered."

She may have been poor, but to Diesel, she was everything he needed and wanted, and he was eager to tell her that.

"Poor is a mentality, Rose. We are rich in ideas. Ideas are given assignments. Those assignments can lead to many things—sometimes misfortune when mishandled, but other times the manifestation of our dreams."

As he talked with ease, Rose sat back and got lost in his words. He was speaking to her, pouring into her sometimes-deflated soul, making her reexamine her outlook on life. Even her purpose.

"And when our dreams became our reality," he said, rinsing out a glass then dropping a few ice cubes in them, "we have fulfilled our purpose, reached our destiny. That shit don't mean we're rich in things or anything like that. It means we did what we were designed to do, to be. Even if that's falling hard... in love."

She laughed, although she wasn't really laughing like something was funny. Love wasn't something she was an expert on, now nodding her head as she looked up to a glass full of her favorite grape juice. The smell, coupled with her scent that included a hint of her sweet-smelling pussy, made him lick his lips.

"Love?" she asked lowly, wanting to hear more as she looked down.

"Yeah. Know anything about that?"

"No," she said, taking a huge gulp of her juice. "It's kind of warm. You're thirsty?" she asked, fanning herself as he chartered into a territory she was a novice in. Well, both actually were, but he knew what he wanted now if he didn't know before.

"Naw, just ready for you to put a dent in that plate so I can give you these meds," he said, noticing she changed the subject so he followed her lead. "May I?" he asked, pointing to her love seat.

"Uh, yeah. It's a little too late to start asking, don't you think?"

He sat and grinned, dropping his head. Rose watched the muscles in his arms flex, the gray T-shirt hugging his broad shoulders and body. He looked good dressed down. Damn good. He had one of the guys at the shop fixing her car—one of his best guys. Taking a shower and getting back to her was all he could focus on.

She looked at his hands and his feet, and he was

huge. With his large stature, Rose felt safe with him. Comfortable and relaxed.

"Eat, crazy girl," he told her when he looked up and smile.

"So I'm a clumsy girl, then a crazy girl. What's next?" she asked, slipping a huge spoon of buttery grits in her mouth.

Mine. I would call you mine.

"Full. You would be full and in bed," he said instead.

Rose sighed, then asked, "Have some?"

"Oh no. Can't. Sort of on a special diet," he said, smiling.

Apparently smiling between the two of them was infectious as she smiled too, dropping her face as she chewed. That's all they did. Smile and took shots at each other, two goofies fighting the pull that could lead them both to love as they got to know each other better.

"I never knew men did the diet thing."

"Yeah, well, some do. Energy drinks are usually my thing. You know, fruit and protein. It's a juicing thing. Juicing is quick. I like juices in my mouth, easy to go down." He felt her energy spike just then and watched her chuckle nervously. His spiked right afterwards, clearing his throat as he rubbed his chest. "I mean, I eat other things, but juicing is fast. I'm always on the go. Anyway, I'm good," he said, feeling himself getting nervous as he started to ramble.

Damn, she has you sounding like a lame.

"Where are your meds?" he asked to recover.

"Right here," she said, holding them up in one hand. "As soon as I take them, I plan to make a few calls and then sort of rest," she said, voice trailing off.

"Oh yeah? Got to call your father, work... some dude?"

"What dude?" she asked with a raised brow, looking up at him. "Thought you told me I didn't have one of those?"

"I was just fucking around and kind of mad if you did have one. Your shit is a classic. I know parts are hard to come by, but if you did have a man, it's his job to make sure you're straight. And working those hours are no joke. I'd shut that down if you were mine," he said with finality, even though it was posed hypothetically, not even realizing this was the first time he spoke freely on laying claim to her out loud.

"So do that then," she said and smiled, shocking her damn self. "Make me yours." She took a drink of the grape juice, forcing him to watch her gulp it down as he struggled to stay put. He could feel her throat contracting and his dick rising to the occasion.

Fuck, I need to go.

"Girl, stop playing. Anyway, I need to get up out of here and get this car. Now," he said, grabbing her medications and pulling them out. She could have felt some type of way when he didn't take her bait, but she caught him blushing, so she was cool with it. "Give me your hand."

"You do know I'm twenty-three, right? Been living alone for some time now."

"Yes, and I know you're clumsy and crazy and procrastinate like your car. We've established that," he said and laughed. "So open up."

She did as he placed one pain pill along with the iron and vitamin D.

"Now down them and let me see the inside of your mouth so I can make sure you swallowed them.

Rose liked recognizing he was a bit nervous. He moved and talked faster when he was nervous. Did this thing, patting his fingers against his leg that she supposed was to calm himself down.

"Ahhhh," she said, opening her mouth so he could see.

Fuck. Fuck. Fuck. Fuck.

"Good girl. Now get some rest, but call your people before you do."

"I did that. Well, not my daddy yet. Not ready to tell him what happened. I loved that car, and he might decide he wants to take it from me. I know it's old, but it has sentimental value to me, you know?"

"Yeah?"

"Yes, it was my mom's," was all she said, sadness enveloping her then consuming him.

He didn't like it at all as he took a deep breath.

"Well, it will be good as new. No need to tell him. I got you."

She perked up when she heard that, and he felt it too. "You really do got me?"

"I mean, haven't I so far?"

"You have," she said with a shrug. "How many other women you have?"

Damn, I didn't see that coming.

"One," he said, feeling her tense up as she shot him a look. "My moms. I love that woman. She's itty bitty like you. Fiesty, too. Probably why I'm digging you," he admitted with ease.

"You're digging me?" she repeated, popping a shrimp in her mouth. That fucking mouth was about to make him have her ass turned around and tooted up for him to feast on it too if she kept it up.

"Yeah, you're a'ight."

"You're such a bad liar. Girls don't like bad liars."

"Oh, so y'all like good ones? Glad to know."

"No, we don't want y'all lying period. That shit is whack and unnecessary. Life is already hard enough trying to make it. The last thing a woman needs is to hear a lie that doesn't have to be told. I'd rather the truth and the truth alone. Even if it means I get hurt."

He wondered if omission was a lie, not sharing who he was, but he had to remain silent. Any word of who they were could jeopardize their existence on Earth or worse, the existence of Earth itself. No way would they allow humans to destroy them, and no way would he'd let Etan keep him from her.

"I hear you. So I'll rap with you later?"

"Yeah, and I forgot to tell you one other thing, too," she said, pouting. "I sort of got laid off. So as soon as you leave, I'm going to call my boss and beg for my job back. Dreams require manifestation, right?" He loved she was listening, fighting back to no matter what he did to help our out. She was reaching out on her own without even mental influence or manipulation from him.

"True that, but never beg a motherfucker for shit, Rose Steel. They should be begging you."

"Well, not beg, but try at least one more time. I know he needs the help."

Luckily for him, he already took care of that for her. He'd just got so caught up kicking it with her that he forgot to ask her about her job.

"Well, shit, call the job now. If the boss man's not trying to work with you, remember, I got you."

"I don't want you going up there handling Mr. Roscoe," she said, busting out laughing. "He's old, Diesel. It's not that serious. I will just eat... whatever. Find a new gig. Life happens," she said, voice trailing off.

Rose, make the fucking call.

"But I will call now because you're right. I have things I need to do, and sitting here feeling sorry for myself won't get me there. One second," she said, reaching for her cell. When she dialed the diner's number, she poked out her lip, giving him a pouty face.

He wanted to take those fucking lips, too, patting his leg with his fingers as she held the cell to her ear.

"Hey, Mr. Roscoe? It's me, Rose. So I was calling to ask you one more time about my—" she said and stopped, mouth popping wide open before turning into a smile.

And there it is. My job is almost done.

"Really? Are you sure?" she asked, looking up at Diesel, full of excitement. "Okay! Sure! Well, not tonight," she said, sneaking a peek his way. "But definitely tomorrow night. Oh my God, Mr. Roscoe! Thank you, thank you, thank you! Okay. See you then. Bye."

Diesel laughed the entire time, feeling her energy unravel and spiral out in waves that increased his own heart rate. Rose was going to definitely be the death of him.

"Diesel, I can't believe this! Man," she said, looking at him, then dropping her eyes.

"What's up, Rose?" he said, feeling her get all emotional. "You can't believe what?" He probed, squatting down in front of her.

Rose couldn't help but feel the closeness, watching his firm thighs and arms as he steadied himself in front of her while her eyes began to water. She hadn't been this close to a man she actually liked in years, almost forgetting what she was about to say. She was grateful for the good news she'd just heard, but even more grateful he was there... with her.

"Oh, so Mr. Roscoe said I could keep my job. Not what I usually do, of course, with the foot thing but stuff like inventory. You know, ordering food stuff. And cleaning up, like loading up the washer. Even some food prep. Basically, anything that won't require me to stand. Isn't that amazing? I start tomorrow night."

No, you're amazing. So fucking amazing.

"It is, Rose. Seems like everything's going to be okay," he said, looking at his watch. It was like time stood still whenever he was with her but sped up and past them by like the speed of lightning.

"Now, all I have to do is get to this shop so you can have your car back by tomorrow."

"You sound like managing life is so easy to do. What if it's more than just that with my car? I mean, it is old."

He sighed, reaching for both of her hands. "Rose, stop it. Life's good. Stop all that worrying and rest your pretty head. A'ight?" He watched her lowkey pout, making him smile.

Cute ass.

"Now, I've taken up more than enough of your time. I've got to get going. I'll have your car dropped off first thing in the morning. And luckily, it's your left foot you hurt, so you should be able to drive. Just not too much. Painkillers might make you sleepy. Go only where you need to go, so get some sleep," he said, sounding like a concerned and protective boyfriend. She wasn't used to that.

He noticed a slight shift in her mood as her face relaxed but nothing to be concerned about.

"Not really," she said lowly. "You really haven't." As soon as he left, she'd be alone again. She didn't want that and he felt it, squeezing both of her hands to reassure he she'd be okay.

"Yes, really, Rose Steel," he said.

"Uh," she said, looking at his huge hands covering hers.

"No worries. I'm gone," he said before he realized what he had done, releasing her hands.

"Later, baby girl."

She grinned, liking that one. *Baby girl.*

"Yes, sir." She smiled sheepishly when she said it, too.

"Naw, not sir. Diesel Weber," he added. "I don't think I told you my last name. You better start checking these niggas, Rose." He knew he was dealing with a woman that was bit more green the average woman he encountered out here in these streets since she wasn't checking him like she should have.

"Which ones?"

"Honestly, it better only be me, so try me. And let meet me know when I'm overstepping," he told her with a smile as he stood.

Damn, he's so fucking fine.

He grinned as he shook his head when he heard that. It made him want to finish what they both started, but instead opened the door, turned the lock, and walked out the door.

8

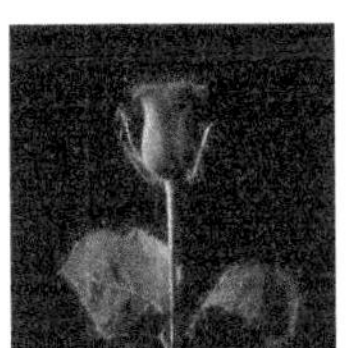

"Miamiiii, let's make some noise for my boy, your hometown R&B swooning ass, singing sensation, Getty Riker! Stand up!" DJ Khaled screamed, raising both hands in the air as the stadium exploded with excitement.

When he was on stage, Getty went by the last name Riker because, let's face it, Moore was boring as hell.

The young girls started screaming and crying while the older women were lifting up their shirts, showing off their breasts. It was a female phenomenon all over the country while Getty's music was in the top ten on the pop and R&B charts.

Diesel would go as often as he could, choosing to remain backstage. While Getty loved the spotlight, Diesel was more of a one-on-one man, enjoying simple interaction like a conversation about everyday life. The paparazzi would go just as wild, fiending for any kind of information they could get on him, but they couldn't.

In fact, Getty's background was untouchable and nearly untraceable, especially being an independent artist. Any news they tried to dig up on Getty were bits and pieces that he and his publicist, Gail, threw their way. She was a young, Jewish bitch that managed to finesse her way backstage one night when he first started performing.

After he hit it a few times, which led to her laying up and actually giving him her resume, he was beyond impressed. He needed her around as long as she minded the business that paid her, and what she didn't mind, he wiped her mind clean.

As far as the media was concerned, Getty was from England and raised in an orphanage but graduated to the streets with a guitar and tin can as he played his music on the streets. They even photoshopped a few photos he tossed Gail's way. She ate it up, and the rest was history.

Not having family ties made staying discreet easier and less stressful when the questions came. And the only family he had to the ones he did business with was Diesel, and he kept it that way.

Getty was still in shock Zara had no clue as to who he was. He wore a dark pair of shades, but a few stares that came his way too long alerted him that his cover may be blown. So having the escape of going home to

Etan did have its benefits. There, no one cared that he could perform his ass off. His music wasn't for enjoyment in Etan. It was a weapon. Hell, a weapon on Earth too when he felt like using it.

"Miami, I see y'all," he said, laughing as the security fought off two women trying to get on stage.

"Getttyyyy, I love youuuu!" one yelled out, face wet with tears. She was hyperventilating, about to fall out with her hair all over her head.

He winked, taking a good look at her breasts bouncing up and down. *Got damn, shit! I might have to get her to the back now.*

As the crowd continued to go wild, Getty started unbuttoning his top. He was a lighter, younger version of Tank. A prettier version too. He knew it as he rubbed his hand slowly down his stomach, slipping it in his pants.

"I want to have your babyyyy!" he heard a woman scream.

"Shit, keep playing, and you might." He laughed, and those in the crowd that heard the exchange laughed too. "Anyway, I'll fuck you properly, and we can chat later about that baby," he told her, gripping his dick. "Aye, Miami! Getty motherfucking Riker is here! Act the fuck up!" he bellowed.

The arena easily filled with twenty thousand people exploded into a loud cry of applause and screams while the lights dimmed and the music started.

Reaching back, he grabbed his guitar, picked it up, and kissed it.

"This my real bitch right here," he told them. "Y'all ready?"

A chorus of "hell yeah" and screams of "ready" could be heard as he started to play. He calmed the crowd down just a little, easing into a nice, slow ballad that hypnotically put the ladies under a spell before he started to sing.

"Last night, I dreamed of youuu. All about you, I was hot, so hot. I needed you and that pussy all up in my spot. Yeah, youuuu. Hell yeah, I'm talking about youuu..."

When a woman fainted, Diesel laughed as he stood on the side of the stage, shaking his head. Most of those lyrics didn't portray how Getty truly felt. If a woman was in his home or in his bed, that was his bitch, his old lady.

Like Getty, for years, not one single woman could identify where Diesel laid his head, and he never rode the same route coming or going home. It was one reason he ran into Rose that night, going a back way to avoid the downtown, late-night club traffic.

While this was the music business, he felt if Getty could write it, he could live it.. No, Diesel hadn't always practiced what he preached, but he hadn't sold a woman a dream either over the years. After Delilah, it took him some time to recover before his parents even allowed him to return to Earth. And not because he was in danger, but because he became self-destructive.

It led to his diet change, eating right, exercising, and throwing himself into work. He always liked doing things with his hands, especially fixing things like bicycles and motorcycles and scooters. He graduated to cars, mostly old ones, but he could practically work on anything you put in front of him with an engine. He could build a plane, too. He was a beast when you put a set of tools in his hands, but when it came to love, now that was sticky.

Love fucked you up. Point blank period.

Sadly, after getting Rose's Mustang fixed as promised, she was a thing of the past. It had been a few weeks, and while it was one of the hardest things he felt he had to do, he decided, for her peace and his sanity, he had to stay away from her.

He even had someone else drop her car off that day. Now, weeks later, he sat surrounded in an arena of tits and ass that any man would indulge in eagerly. Any man, yet he wasn't enthused. He'd had his dick sucked by randoms on demand a few days after work just to release his frustrations, but he still wasn't satisfied. Each time, he dismissed them as soon as he bust a hot one down their throat, thinking of Rose. He wanted something more meaningful, and no one except Rose would do.

He was sure of it.

Once he grew bored and got tired of the woman losing their minds over his whack ass best friend, Diesel headed back to Getty's dressing room. No matter where he performed, they spared no expense. It was set up like a hotel suite, complete with a bar, flat-screen TV, and plush furniture, like a sofa and lounge chair next to the small dressing section.

Getty wasn't with all the makeup, but he kept his Mohawk tight by bringing his barber with him on the road. Scooby, as they called him, was cool as fuck. He didn't talk much, just came to cut Getty's head, and took off until he was called again.

Once Diesel made it to the dressing room, he pulled out his cell, tapped on his HBO Go app, and found *Game of Thrones*.

"This my shit," he said and smiled, settling in on the sofa that was in there.

He enjoyed the action, the savage-like moves he saw that kept everyone addicted to the show week after week, even him. He didn't want to think about Rose or else he'd be in a fucked-up mood.

An hour and half later, Getty came through the door sweaty and grinning like he was ready to fuck something.

"Boy, did you see all that ass out there?" Getty shouted, wiping his face and neck with a hand towel. "D, you got to get in on this. I got three ready. I mean, *ready*, ready!"

His security just chuckled. They weren't friends, but he kept a few on the payroll just to manage the influx of women that might come through during a show.

Outside of Diesel, there was no entourage sucking off of his earnings or sipping off bottles of liquor in the club. In fact, Getty hated them, preferring private hotel parties with a gang of women only.

"Three? Why three?"

"Two for me, and one for you. Shoot, I know you can't handle more than one, but you know me! I'm putting in that work!"

Waving him off, Diesel sat back and wondered what Rose was doing right now. It was close to midnight on a Friday night. She had her car back, so hitting the streets wasn't totally out of the question, but he hoped she was wrapping up at the diner and heading home. But even then, she could still step out. He got a peek at her home girl Zara. It didn't take long for him to see she was the wild, rebel out to the two of them, getting agitated the more he thought about it.

Naw, she need to sit her clumsy ass right the fuck at home... alone.

"Don't," Getty said, sucking his teeth as he prepared for a quick shower. He already knew he was mulling over not seeing Rose.

They'd talked about it, and honestly, Getty was glad. He even decided to make that made-up situation with

Zara a thing of the past. She was dangerous, making him trip the way he did after tasting the pussy once.

"Just don't. Didn't I just say we got pussy, three of them waiting? Come on, D."

"Stay out of my fucking head, Getty," he shot back.

"Look, all I'm saying is, for one night, do something different. You were trying not to come tonight. And I already know you was watching some shit on that fucking app during my show."

"Why not? I heard all of them same ass songs and have watched the same thing happen in every city from here to LA. Same thing, G. The same fucking thing."

"Which is exactly why getting in on this is something different! Now, I'm going to shower. When I come out, put your game face on. Remember, these girls won't remember a thing once we hit it and send them on their way."

Nodding his head, Diesel somewhat committed to following Getty's lead. Other than fixing cars, he didn't do much, but most nights, besides watching TV or visiting Etan to check in on his parents. He did like to bowl, but Getty told him bowling was for bitches that liked getting fucked in the ass. He didn't even debate it. Getty always went to the extreme on everything, so he didn't bother,

While Getty was in the shower, Diesel decided he needed a moment, just one moment, to see Rose. Not talk to her, but see her to get his mind focused or at least enough to not think about her when he linked up with whoever Getty had for him. Within seconds, he was standing outside of her apartment. A second later, he was on the second floor and next second, in her apartment. A light was on, alerting him she was up.

Impulsively, he went inside, immediately veiling himself to become invisible. The living room was dark and quiet, but the light where she was called him. He wanted to run and leap on her after hearing her soft giggle coming from her bedroom.

"Stop it, Zara! No way, na uh," she said, covering her mouth.

Diesel took off, making his way down the hall. When he got to her room, he'd almost lost it, watching her in a tiny T-shirt and bikini underwear laying on the bed. Her smooth skin and the muscle tone that was well defined when she stretched set his body on fire. He couldn't help but notice her nipples, hard and firm, pressing against the thin material of her shirt.

"Hold on, girl. It's just got warm in here," she said, sitting up.

What Diesel saw next was the final confirmation Rose had him. As she crossed and wiggled her arms just enough to pull her top off, his eyes moved erratically. With each tug as her shirt came up, his member grew long and thick as he lusted over her petite body.

Fuck, you're beautiful. He couldn't help but notice the

rose tattoo that sat just above her tiny breast on the left side.

"That's better. I gotta call the landlord or something. Wait, let me check the thermostat."

As she got up, he watched her tiny yet firm and round hips from behind as she stepped out into the hallway. She was definitely not Getty's taste, but she was perfectly made just for him.

He followed her, although he knew he shouldn't have and stood behind her. With a slow lift of his hand, he softly lifted her hair that hung over her shoulder and inhaled.

Fuck it. That's it. I'm staying. I'm staying here tonight.

"What the—" she said to herself, spinning around, now facing him. Her eyes darted around, but she didn't move as she surveyed the hallway. Then she took slow steps toward the living room, peeking out just enough before she flicked the light on. "Shoot, I'm tripping. I must be catching the flu or something. Got me feeling things."

I'd gladly catch that flu. Damn it, Rose. Please put some fucking clothes on. I can't take it.

Turning off the light, Rose swiftly walked back to her room and picked up her cell. "Yeah, girl. It's not the thermostat. It's on sixty-nine," she said, causing Diesel to bite his lip.

He was quite familiar with the sixty-nine but felt Rose's lips were too pretty and precious to have a dick in her mouth. If she were his, he'd just want to kiss them and make love to her mouth with his.

"Uh no!" she squealed, laughing loudly as she covered her mouth. "I have not used it."

Used what?

"Because, Zara, it's—it's unnatural. A woman is supposed to receive pleasure from her mate, man, or whatever he or she is supposed to be these days. And clearly, I don't have one."

He'd be fucking dead. I'd kill him before he could touch you. Diesel knew he was pushing it. *Stop it, Diesel. You can't. She wants to be a doctor. She's smart and beautiful and wants to save lives through medicine the RIGHT way, not through the means of eradicating evil people by way of death.*

"Well, I didn't ask you to buy it. Hell, you didn't even give it to me. You stashed that big ole thing in my book bag! No, I won't. Whatever," she said, sticking her tongue out, even though Zara couldn't see her. "Alright. Get one in for me. Bye, bitch!" she and laughed, shaking her head.

She lay there for a few minutes stretching, as she got comfortable. She was used to sleeping alone, even not having a man, but as of late, she was starting to feel and think very sexually. Masturbation wasn't her thing, but the longer she lay there, the stronger the urge grew. Once the urge did, she mumbled, "Maybe I should try it out."

Run, get the hell up out of here. Or you will never want to leave her. He could smell her clean pussy already, and she hadn't even touched it yet.

"Naw, this is silly," she said, nipples sitting up erect like plump raisins.

His mouth watered as he struggled to will her to cover them up. Yet he didn't, almost in a trance.

"Oh, what the hell," she said, sitting up and opening the nightstand drawer next to her bed.

There he saw a journal, that journal he wanted to take so bad. He knew it was a cheat sheet to her secrets and her soul, but without looking, he felt their souls were already connected. Had to be if he was there now and not back with Getty to get some ass.

As he fought with himself, she pulled out this massive, fucking hot-pink dildo. It was huge with rabbit ears that twirled attached to it.

As her eyes widened, he almost stopped breathing. He wasn't sure if he wanted her to give it a try or if he wanted to destroy it, knowing it would soon be inside of her, pleasuring her.

"So I guess this is where I turn this thing on."

He watched her turn the handle upside down, then press a button.

"Oh, shoot!" she gasped, feeling a slow vibration shoot up her hand. "And that's low? Sheesh!"

Ah, what the hell. Lay back down on your back and open your legs.

And she did, slowly taking off her panties first, giving him a show as if she knew he was there watching and waiting. Diesel bit his lip. Her scent overwhelmed his nasal passage as he sniffed the air in the room like a dog in heat. Inhaling her, Diesel was beyond two moons high.

Open your thighs and those lips, sweetheart. Spread them slowly for me.

Rose immediately placed the dildo to her side on the bed, then dropped her legs to each side, taking a deep breath. He watched her stomach go in and out and in and out as she built up the courage to pleasure what he deemed his pussy.

Slowly, she lifted her right hand, sliding down her stomach that seemed to quake, releasing a hiss from her mouth when it landed on top of her second set of lips.

That's it, baby girl. Let me see that pussy.

"Uh," she uttered, separating them as her already-engorged clitoris sat up under the hood that glistened.

After she spread them, he watched her inner lips swell as the blood rushed to them. She was wet, so wet. Her pussy bloomed like a flower as the scent consumed the room.

Got damn it, Rose.

A soft, glistening fluid appeared, even before she touched herself. Her eyes were closed, but she was very much in tune with what her body felt.

Taking a slender, index finger, Rose touched her

yoni and gasped, her back shooting up like her body was struck by lightning. "Uh! Uh! Uhhh."

Yes, baby girl. Slowly circle around it. Yes, just like that.

By this time, Diesel was almost on top of her but would never touch her, hovering over her body. Watching her, being closer to her, inhaling her. It was better than someone painting an exquisite portrait of great value. Rose, with the way her body contorted and responded to his commands, was more priceless than any body of work. She was art.

She bit and sucked her lips as her eyes batted, then squeezed tightly. Her areolas responded to her touch on demand. Her breasts were small but more than enough to fill his mouth and one day feed his babies.

He traveled down to her stomach and her hips, hips he wanted to spread so he could partake of the paradise existing between them, showering down a stream of her goodness he ached to taste. The way she moved her body forced him to steady himself as he was close to exploding when her eyes popped open wide, staring into his.

Even though he was still invisible, it was as if she knew he was there, begging and pleading with her lips and eyes that pooled with tears to touch, to have his way with her.

Once he saw she was about to lose control, he stopped her. He wanted to see how tight she was, praying it was so fucking tight that he'd bust a hot one from watching.

Pick it up and slide it down your body and into my pussy, Rose.

"Oh, shit," she huffed, stopping and looking to her left. She quickly picked the dildo up, but this time, she saw there was a second button for the rabbit ears. They were attached to stimulate her clitoris. Then she stopped, panic setting in. She was intimidated, second-guessing herself.

"I can't," she whispered, her breathing slowing down as the euphoric feeling began to subside.

Try it, baby. Try for me, please.

"Of course I can," she said to herself, laughing nervously. She wrinkled her nose again as she answered him and herself without even knowing. "If I don't like it, I can just stop, right?"

Oh, you're going to fucking love it. Shit, I love it already, and you ain't even used it yet.

Diesel was stroking his joint, chewing the hell out of his lip as he waited anxiously for her to put that dildo to work. Turning it on, she took a deep breath and slowly lay back down, spreading her legs wide. So wide that her right leg as almost hung off of the bed. Positioned at the foot of her bed, Diesel slowed his stroke down, breathing in sync with her.

It's okay, baby girl. Do it. Do it for me.

Watching the rabbit ears vibrate, Rose peered over

her belly cautiously as she lowered them to her leaking center.

"Oh, shit!" she spat, then laughed as she dropped her head back.

Diesel shot up too as arched her back and cried out.

"Oh my fucking God." Then what she said next drew him closer. "Diesel, baby," she hissed.

What? Me, sweetheart?

Lying back down, she took another deep breath and lowered her legs gasping when the ears touched her the opening of her love. "Mmmmm, Diesel," she moaned. "Ahhhh, yes. Suck your pussy, baby. Uh, mmm."

Keep fucking around, and I will. Now keep going. And she did.

Diesel watched her face contort, her hips winding slowly while the dildo sat at the mouth of her pretty pussy. The vibration of the rabbit ears was powerful, feeling the effects of them touching her body. The contrast of her pink center against chocolate skin was mesmerizing. Diesel groaned, feeling the pressure build up in his loins. He wanted to suck and fuck her so bad.

Push it in, now.

With a forceful push, Rose stretched herself wide, then cried out, "Fuckkkk! Oh, Diesel. Shit, oh my. Shit!"

That's it, keep going. Diesel coached her like a coach on the sidelines of the NBA finals championship game as a team player held the ball with only ten seconds left and a tied game. It was tight very tight, but as she worked it in and out slowly, swirling those baby-making hips, it loosened up. Her calling his name made it personal for her and life-changing for him. She was the prize, the only prize, and all roads led to him.

Diesel refused to look down at himself about to explode. Everything she felt, he felt. Everything she didn't say but thought, he heard. His baby was about to shoot the winning pass as she shot up and screamed. The release spiraled out of control from her pulsating center of gushiness all throughout her body.

"Uh, uh," she groaned as it refused to stop. Her chest heaved as she tried to catch her breath. "Diesel, fuck, baby. Oh, Diesel. Damn you," she grunted lowly. Her high finally came down as she opened her eyes, staring straight in his direction.

If Diesel didn't know any better, he would have thought she could see him, but he knew she didn't when she plopped back onto the bed. The dildo still buzzed as the rabbit ears spiraled around and around.

He groaned inwardly, now hovering over her. His seed expelled as he caught it in his hand, but it was so much, too much. Afraid he couldn't keep it together much longer and accidentally revealing his presence, Diesel immediately left, placing himself back into dressing room bathroom.

He stared at himself in the mirror, sweaty as hell. He took a few deep breaths, waiting until they evened out before he turned on the water to wash and clean himself up. “That was crazy, damn,” he said to himself, grabbing a towel to dry himself off.

He wasn’t sure how long he was gone, but he had to get back out there before Getty recognized he’d slipped up. They had a deal he pretty much lost, but if asked, he would tell him it was worth it. Rose was so fucking hot to him. He could still smell her.

Fixing his clothes as he tucked zipped up his jeans and secured his belt, Diesel took one look at himself to make sure he looked normal. Well, at least he’d act normal.

When he stepped out, there was Getty, staring at him and smirking.

“What? A nigga can’t shit?” he replied with both hands raised up as he lied. He knew he looked and sounded guilty. Besides, Diesel was way too private to use the bathroom there when he could have shot home really quickly.

“Nothing, D. Let’s go,” was all Getty said when he realized they had company.

“Oh, what's up,” he asked the ladies, then shot Getty a look.

You owe me. Now I won.. And because I will play and act like I don’t know, do me a solid and just fuck on her tonight. Show the girl a good time. Hell, I want to see and feel some pussy just like you did.

If Getty knew what he really did, he would have

known he hadn't felt any pussy, but Diesel decided to take that L and just get the night over with. Besides, one sniff of Rose and Getty felt he did anyway, shaking his head.

"Ladies, this is my brother, Diesel. Diesel, the ladies."

These bitches don't have names? Diesel asked him.

Damn their names. I'm not fucking the alphabet. Getty shot Diesel a look telling him to chill out, so he did, shaking his head.

"Ladies, this way," Getty replied, reaching for two, one under each arm. "And you, dear, have this one all to yourself," he said to the third one who was looking at Diesel like she'd won a few lottos and maybe in her eyes she had.

She was the average Miami groupie chick—big hair, big ass, wearing cheap, trendy clothes that left nothing to wonder about. He never understood why a woman felt the need to promote her body, then expect a man to respect it. He was all for confidence, but some things a man should be required to earn. Little mama was losing already as he barely looked at her.

He thought of his mother. She was a classic beauty yet still turned heads. He understood why his father chose her and found himself thinking of Rose, who was a borderline plain Jane woman that exuded a natural sex appeal he could fuck with, and a lot at that. If Rose even thought about wearing this rainbow-colored, see-through outfit this broad had on, he'd blind the whole world.

"Hey, you. I'm Leechie," she said, giggling as she wrapped her arms around him.

Short of her dark complexion, Diesel found nothing attractive about her. In fact, her cheap perfume smelled like roach spray, and her butterfly eyelashes were hideous as hell.

By the time they hit the limo and were popping cheap bottles of Moscato, because Getty was cheap as hell when it came to women, Diesel was over the night already.

"We're here, sir," the driver said almost twenty minutes later as they pulled up to the La Quinta Inn.

Diesel laughed, looking Getty's way. *Cheap ass.*

So, we won't be sleeping anyway. Getty figured why he had to ball out with the likes of these three who were clapping with excitement anyway.

Now that roach spray perfume, flea market hair and clothes made since, Diesel supposed.

"Grab a bottle, ladies, and leave your panties," he told them, smoking a fat cigar as he had one hand in his pants, cupping his balls. "Naw ain't you ready," he hissed as the second one unzipped his pants down further, rubbing his length.

"Oh yes." She laughed, ready to take him in her mouth.

"Now come on, Tic Tac," he called her. Diesel

figured she got the name from not only her breath but because of the rat-sized teeth she was rocking.

Her friend agreed. "Tic Tac, chill. We have all night, right?" she cooed, licking Diesel's ear. She wasn't as bad looking as her friend, but clearly, she didn't know a bra from a slingshot as her breasts rested on her stomach.

"This dude is whack," Diesel grumbled, looking over at Leechie, who was squirming in her seat. "Ayo, G. Let's go."

The paparazzi was everywhere, and while he wasn't a celebrity, he didn't want to be caught out here doing anything that could come back to haunt him. Sure, he could kill them, but why when he could just avoid it?

Once they entered the hotel and their respective rooms, Diesel stopped and looked at Leechie and frowned.

"What's wrong, baby? I don't bite. I swear. I'm just ready to have some fun." Shimmering as she wiggled out of her dress, she turned around and licked her shiny, big nipples one at a time. That was confirmation live and in color that bras hadn't helped her over the years either.

There was no way he was touching her. Getty had to be smoking more than a cigar.

You're tired. Very tired. In fact, your ass has a headache. A big one. It's pounding. I'm talking about pounding for real. You need to lay down and get some rest.

"Oh, no. My head is killing me," she complained

like it came out of nowhere, rubbing both temples. "Wow, I don't know what happened," she said, looking at him confused. "You mind if I lie down for a minute?"

"Naw, do your thing," he said, taking a seat on a nearby sofa. "The bed is yours. I'll be here whenever you're ready."

Leechie didn't even take the time to pull her dress back up, shuffling as it hung around her ankles. From the back, she looked a little better but not enough to reverse the spell he'd just cast on her.

As soon as her head hit the pillow, she was snoring like a grown man. And just like that, Diesel got to relax, leaning his head back with dreams of Rose while Getty blew two bitches' backs out, just like he had planned.

9

Zara tried to sleep, hoping Hugh came in late like he normally would.. That head he gave her in her sleep a few nights ago wasn't the same as what she had a few weeks back. She kept waiting and waiting to feel that immeasurable high, then eruption, but he never seemed to get it right.

She chalked it up to her being worked up about her plans to dump him. It was weighing heavily on her, and she was nearing her wits' end. She was close to telling him, but every single time she was about to, she remembered one thing. He saved her mother's life, and she was in remission from breast cancer for almost five years.

Hugh, barely home most days, had been working on his scientific research he wanted to present to the hospital chair. It was about the restoration of cells destroyed by chemotherapy for cancer patients. While he may have been dull in bed, Zara couldn't help but find his vigor and passion for medicine sexy on some level.

He spent nights on end using donated animal cells for research but hadn't made much leeway, which was frustrating. He thought about Dr. Lee, another well-renowned doctor who specialized in orthopedics.

His research was related to creating lightweight yet steel-like apparatuses that could be used as a prosthetics for arms or legs. But then he wanted to take it a step further, creating those same prosthetics where human veins, cartilage, and muscles could become one with it, never having to come off.

There were a few other physicians with great ideas that could generate tons of money for the hospital, but Dr. Lee's research seemed to draw great interest from the medical community. Every NBA, NFL, or MBA medical doctor across the country flew in to gain more knowledge about it, even had their organizations contributing money for more research.

Hugh was livid. It wasn't like he wasn't receiving donations, but they paled in comparison to Dr. Lee's, making his frustration spill over into his personal life. He was always number one in everything he did, and getting Zara was like icing on the cake. As she lay there, he smiled, taking her in.

He imagined their kids having her sandy-brown hair and warm, creamy skin. Her pouty lips and button nose, too. He was quite the looker himself, fit with firm abs and legs and arms well defined from working out with her. He had to being ten years her senior. His skin complexion was just a bit darker, a soft caramel. Their children would be absolutely gorgeous.

Before her, he was the ladies' man. At Harvard, he had them in and out of his apartment in droves, especially the white girls—cooking, cleaning, and sucking his dick, knowing it wasn't the largest. To them, they were used to it, even though he was smaller than other black men.

That was why it actually surprised him he could even please a woman like Zara. And it was why he worked so hard making sure she received the sloppiest, nastiest head she'd ever had.

"Sweetheart, are you up?" he asked, just wanting to talk.

Zara flinched just a little, pretending he'd just woken her up. She was hoping he'd go to sleep so she could get herself off, but so much for wishful thinking. She slowly opened her eyes, then yawned, covering her mouth.

"I am now. What time is it?" she asked as she fake yawned and stretched.

"Two. Sorry. I tried calling, but you didn't answer."

Zara saw his calls coming, but she was talking to Rose. They had a girls' trip planned at the end of the semester. Nothing extravagant since Rose was always counting every penny, but anything away from Miami, even down to the Keys, was better than nothing.

"Oh, it must be on silent. I came home, popped a Tylenol, and got in bed. Bad cramps," she said, rubbing her belly. Fortunately for her, it *was* that time of the month, but throwing cramps in there meant she didn't have to suck his dick.

"Damn, it is that time," he said under his breath, his small member still firm, needing a release. "Just started?"

"Oh, yeah," she said quickly, regretting it as soon as she did.

Knowing Hugh, he'd still want to have sex, but tonight he surprised her and left her alone. He was starting to go down deep into a rabbit hole. The past few days out of town hadn't gone so well, and he slipped up, remembering we he'd almost got caught.

"Shit," Hugh groaned in her ear, playing in her ass as he stroked her.

Unlike Zara, it took him some time to release when it came to Agnes. That was her first name. It fit her too. She wasn't as exotic as Zara, sort of mousy looking with glasses that she even slept in most of the time after a long day of research.

She didn't care much for fashion, and it showed. Yet she had a body, one that Hugh noticed one night when they were working in lab. Agnes believed in him, sometimes he felt more than Zara had. She would get to the hospital early and stay late. In between, she would email him scholarly articles for him to look at.

To her, molecular cell regeneration was exciting. She could indulge in it all day, captivating Hugh, who was fascinated with her dedication to his case. They'd been at it all day, and Zara was out with Rose, or so she told him. He was starving and decided to grab a bite to eat on his way home. As a kind gesture, and because he didn't like to eat alone, he invited Agnes, who gladly accepted.

As she walked, she wobbled with feet sore from standing all day. When she refused to take her shoes off, Hugh offered her his arm to steady her as she took it. Instantly, she felt a rush of excitement but not the kind she did when it came to medicine. No, this was the kind only a man could elicit, a man she'd been pining over silently for years.

They went to La Caretta, a Spanish restaurant with live music and dancing. After eating mounds of steak, sweet plantains, black beans, and rice, Agnes was stuffed, but Hugh refused to leave until he treated her to a bottle of wine.

"Oh, Hugh. It's late. We have an early day tomorrow." She laughed, shaking her head as he poured her a glass of merlot.

"Are you always this focused...disciplined?" he asked, placing the bottle down.

By now, she'd loosened the bun that held her hair together, causing it to fall on her shoulders. It wasn't intentional, but instead up fixing it, Hugh told her to leave it down.

"If you mean how serious I take medicine, then the answer is yes. It's who I am and what I do. Certainly, you are too. Look at all of your awards, the accolades you receive." She laughed, then dropped her head. She couldn't stare at him for too long with no distraction, fearing he'd noticed the effect he had on her.

"I am, but I also know life needs balance, Agnes. Come," he said, standing up and reaching for her hand. "Let's dance."

"Oh, I don't dance," she said quickly.

"Well, follow my lead. You seem to trust me," he said, hoping she did.

"Of course, but no laughing, and any word of this to our colleagues, and I will swear to them that you're lying," she told him, getting up.

"Leave off the shoes. Besides, I like your feet," he said. He noticed them when he forced her to come out of them once they sat down.

After two sets and polishing off two bottles of wine, Hugh had fucked every hole that Agnes had in the back of his truck. Then when they got to her place, he just couldn't leave, following her in, where they woke up in each other's arms. Sadly, when he reached for his cell, he had not one missed call from Zara.

He kissed her long and hard, apologizing before he left. They both blamed it on the alcohol, but for months, they indulged in sex, whether they were drunk or not. Agnes was on cloud nine until the calls after work started coming in less. Then they weren't returned at all.

At that time, she knew nothing of a fiancée, but she soon found out. It was Valentine's Day weekend, and she had a whole weekend planned. Hugh promised to meet up with her Friday night, where she had two tickets to go to Costa Rica, and he never showed up.

Unable to sleep, Agnes got worried, hoping he was okay. Especially when his cell continuously went to voicemail. She'd been by his place before when they both started working at the university's hospital. Hugh was new, and this was his way of breaking the ice with his colleagues. Sadly for him, Agnes still had his address saved in her cell.

"Yes, he's here," she whispered to herself, parking in his driveway. She noticed a car she'd never seen him drive before but ignored it. It was a red Maserati with extremely dark tints. She figured it was something he only drove on the weekends. Walking quickly past it, she walked up to the door and rang the doorbell.

She heard him yell, "I got it! It's probably the dress!"

The dress? she asked herself, wondering what dress he would need and for who. "Hmph, maybe it's his sister," she said, remembering him mentioning one—a needy one at that. Eager to see him, she got anxious as she waited for him to open the door.

"Well—oh," he said, stepping out quickly and closing the door behind him. "Dr. Kemp? Is everything okay?"

She wasn't sure since he never called her Dr. Kemp when they were alone but dismissed it as she went in for a kiss. He laughed, turning his head as he leaned and looked through his living room window.

"She's sick," he whispered. "My sister. She's very sick, coughing all night. Not sure what it is," he lied, quickly leading her back to her car.

"Oh," she said more to herself, remembering him yell about a dress. "Well, is there anything I can do?" she asked, stopping him. "I can go get soup, cough drops, lemon, honey —you name it."

"Actually, Agnes," he said, knowing he didn't have much time. "You see, I really like you."

"Great, I like you too." She laughed nervously yet felt a lump in her throat when she did. "And the time we spend together."

"Wonderful, but you know with us working together so closely—"

"Hugh, baby? Everything's okay?" a younger woman asked at the door, her face feigning confusion.

She looked familiar to Agnes, but she couldn't place why as she stepped out onto the porch.

"Zara, my love. Yes, yes, of course. Dr. Kemp forgot our meeting was canceled tonight. Apparently, I hadn't been picking up, so, on her way home, she decided to stop by and check on me."

"Oh, okay," she replied, wondering what meeting they would have planned right before Valentine's Day. "Hey, Dr. Kemp! I'm Zara. Nice to meet you! You know Hugh can be

very forgetful. Thanks for stopping by and letting him know, and Hugh, hurry up," she said, going back inside.

"Go, please. I promise I will explain everything to you later." Hugh felt like shit, being met with the saddest eyes.

He really did like Agnes, but she just couldn't be his leading lady, because she just didn't fit the part.

"Agnes, I really do like you," he said, meaning it.

"Well, clearly enough to lie."

"Not about how I feel," he replied quickly, grabbing her by both shoulders. "When I get some time to tell you what this all about, I promise you will understand. Just don't shut me out... please."

"Very well," she said, clearing her throat as her eyes misted up—the softest, brown eyes that complemented her mahogany complexion. She even started getting her hair done, wearing a blunt, edgy bob.

"I love you," he said before she walked away.

"Yeah, Hugh. I love you, too."

Hugh had just found out that not only was Dr. Kemp no longer working with him on his research, but she was now chief of staff and, unofficially, dating Dr. Lee. It made him go back and forth, wondering if this was a sign to finally do something that had nothing to do with status but with his heart.

For the first time in almost five years, he looked at his fiancée and wished she was anywhere but there.

10

After Rose's foot had healed up nicely, she was back to her regular routine, working even more hours. It nagged her, however, that every time she sat in her Mustang, she thought of Diesel.

She could swear it even had a softer hum it, riding smoother than it had ever run before. Her father credited it to the work he had done on it after Diesel had it returned, but she would never tell him. She loved her daddy too much for that.

Today, her schedule had changed since her lab class had been canceled. With no other classes for the rest of the day, she decided to hit Zara up.

"Hey, what's up, girl?"

"Hey, Rosey. You snuck out of labs?" she asked, giggling in a sneaky way.

"What?"

"Mine just started," she whispered. "You want me to sneak out, too?"

Rose pulled her cell away and shook her head. "Oh, it is your lab day, too. I'm so sorry. Call me later."

"No, no. You're okay?"

"Girl, yeah. Mine was canceled."

"Then I am sneaking out. Wait for me."

"Bye, Zara," she said, hanging up on her. There was no way she would encourage that. Besides, she had plenty of studying too and was already behind. Just as she pulled off to head to the library, her cell rang. It was Zara, calling right back.

"Zara, I was only trying to see what you were doing tonight?" she whispered as if she were in class. "It's Thursday. I'm off tonight."

"No studying? Damn."

"Wait, did you walk out of class?"

"It's called a bathroom break, Rose. Pull your thong out your ass," she told her, still bummed about her uneventful life. She looked for anything that could spice it up, the wheels spinning in her head as she pushed in the bathroom door.

"Anyway, it's nothing. I was about to study. Probably should have thought of that before I called you," she told her, sighing.

Unlike Rose, Zara didn't have to study. She was just that astute. She could cram the night before, ace the test, and mess up the grading curve. Rose wasn't jealous at all. She just knew that to get what Zara got, she had to do something different and more of it like study.

"Too late," she told her, speaking with her cell on speaker as she scrolled through it. "There's this spot I want to check out. They have live music, a Caribbean menu, and five-dollar mojitos, Long Island iced teas, and sex on the beach. They just opened up a week ago in midtown. Let me call you after labs so we can discuss."

"Mmmm, midtown. Okay, we'll chat then."

Rose hung up, deflated. She realized she was indeed a geek. She realized she was indeed a geek, and her life was boring and predictable, so Rose decided to hop in her Mustang and go see her daddy instead. They had the talk about boys years ago when Rose was in high school, but it was really for nothing. The guys weren't checking for her like that, but no one could tell Mr. Eddie that. To him, Rose was the prettiest thing, and any boy would be lucky to get a shot with his little girl. Especially the ones who dumped her once their tutoring was done or they realized trying to get her in bed was too time consuming.

It was just before eleven, but if she hurried, she'd have time to go to the Cuban bakery and grab him some breakfast.

"Yes, Daddy's going to be so surprised," she said snickering as she mashed the gas.

11

Diesel was a morning person. Always had been. Even as a kid. Like clockwork, he'd get up and say his morning prayers, wash up, get dressed, and take off mostly alone but on some days with Getty. With him in the studio all times of night, that happened less often, but he liked being alone. It gave him time to reflect and beat himself up about what he did to Rose.

She might not have known it, but he did. That was almost two months ago, and he felt he'd finally gotten her out of his system. He did everything he could to not drive by the diner or take the route he took the night they'd met. He didn't even go near her neighborhood if he could help it, feeling stronger and stronger every day.

"Good morning, Sunshine," April said to him as he

pulled up to the shop. Her and her husband's pawnshop was right next door.

He smirked, shaking his head. "What I told you about calling me that, April? That sounds like some bitch boy shit, girl."

"Ahhh, you know you like it. I see you smiling," she cooed, waving at him.

"Actually, I don't. And it's early, the sun's barely out. You trying to get robbed, huh?" he asked, getting out of his truck, then locked it.

"Nope. It's Thursday. Thursdays are always my busiest days. Folks got bills to pay on Friday, especially payday Friday. But this one isn't, so you already know the goods are about to start coming in. Everyone ain't so lucky to own their own business, you know," she said to him, batting her eyes as she nudged his shoulder.

"Where's Bean?" he asked, hoping she remembered she had a man.

"Coming, but you know Bean," she said with a frown on his face. "Late night at the pool hall. That man spend money as soon as we make it. What kind of backward ass shit is that?"

Diesel knew she was complaining, trying to get some sympathy conversation, but he liked Bean, and business was most definitely good next door.

People pawned almost anything, and Bean was a businessman. If he could find a way to resell it elsewhere, instead of leaving it in his shop once the owner never came back, he did, and he did it at the pool hall. To Diesel, April was lucky she'd caught and locked down a legal hustler. She just didn't know it.

"Yeah, well, knowing Bean, he won a few dollars. And what he didn't, he sold a few things. Let his ass make it," he said to her with a soft smile as he did Bean a solid.

"Yeah, I guess," she said when she was really thinking, *fuck Bean.*

Diesel pulled up the garage door, giving it a light push until it rolled all the way up. Thursdays were his busy days, too, trying to get cars out of there before the influx of repairs that came in on the weekends.

April watched the firm, muscles in his arms and slightly bowed legs in his work pants. She couldn't keep her eyes off of Diesel. She wasn't a bad-looking girl herself, but she was definitely not one Diesel wanted to get down with. With butterfly, glued-on eyelashes, and a few bundles of sewn-in weave, April was fifty percent unnatural all the way down to her ass that was too big and a tad bit on the lumpy side.

Diesel wondered why she got butt shots if that was the end result, but it wasn't his business since it was Bean hitting that defective ass. Her skin, however, was a flawless mocha color that he did take a liking to, but his likes stopped right there.

She wasn't getting any dick, and she couldn't suck him off.

"Hungry?" she asked, following him inside. "I was about to run up the street to the Cuban bakery."

Shit, this fucking girl won't leave me alone.

And even though she wouldn't, he realized he really was hungry. He made a small pot of warm wala this morning but hadn't juiced or made anything to put on his stomach.

Besides, Diesel was too kind and mannerable to insult her since for the most part she was cool, so instead of telling her to fuck off like he another woman trying to get at, he turned around and smiled instead. When he did, her eyes landed on his private parts, and a smile stretched widely across her face.

He didn't even want to know what she was thinking, immediately blocking out her thoughts. It still didn't matter, though, since it was plastered all over her face. She definitely wanted to fuck.

It's too fucking early for this bullshit.

When he heard his stomach grumble, he decided it couldn't hurt. They would be in public and not alone anyway.

"Sure, I could use a breakfast smoothie, but let me finish opening up," he said, moving around to turn on the lights. The other two guys he had, Chill and Dank, wouldn't be in for another hour or two.

Chill was married to his high-school sweetheart with three kids, and Dank was like Diesel—single, except he wanted to be. After a bad divorce, Dank wasn't looking to settle down. They, outside of Getty, were his closest friends and had formed their own small brotherhood.

Chill was a felon he hired who came desperately looking for a job right after release. While locked down, he picked up mechanics as a trade. Dank came a year later when Diesel put up a help wanted sign.

He'd been in business now for ten years. His shop was small but reputable and kept him busy. He loved Etan, but here on Earth, helping others who weren't like him, made him feel valuable and useful.

Chill and Dank used to tease him about being gay early on because they never saw him with a woman. Then, when they realized he'd just hit a few and keep it moving, they eased up on him. Good thing they did because he was close to fucking them up. A few times, they had asked about the mystery owner of the Mustang, and he'd shut them down. Now, he spent his days shutting his own urges down as April walked closely next time him, her arm brushing up against his.

"A little nippy," he said to her, watching as the tight shirt she wore that hid nothing. He could smell her cheap perfume too, hoping she'd use a few ends and buy her a decent bottle of perfume.

"Well, I'm from New York," she reminded him. "This here weather ain't nothing to me."

It wasn't anything to him either, but Diesel preferred his woman only showing their womanly parts to him as their man, clothed or naked. He was somewhat old-fashioned.

"Smells good," he said as they approached the bakery.

They could go to the window and order from there, but going inside would hopefully cause her nipples to return to their normal size.

I ain't trying to see that shit.

Opening the front door and motioning her inside, April grinned as if they were on a date. He'd never do no underhanded shit like that, but he wouldn't say that to her. He already received the "ugly-girl syndrome" tease from Getty sometimes, but he didn't care.

"Oooh, it's warm in here. Good thing you have on short sleeves," she said as they waited to be seated.

In seconds, they sat as he slid in on one side of the booth. While he pretended to go through the menu, even though he knew what he wanted, April didn't. Instead, she was studying him. He couldn't help but grimace, hearing how she wanted to suck the skin off his dick in her head no matter how hard he tried not to. He was antsy now, distracted even. So it made it hard for him to stay focus.

"Ma'am," he called out to the waitress, trying to hurry this along.

He made a note to himself to put Dank on her if she felt compelled to mess around on her man. Dank wasn't selective, and April was ready. A perfect match. If you were into having meaningless sex, he was too.

"Man, I'm so hungry." He faked a stretch, almost standing up to get their order in faster by waving the waitress over there.

"I see." April took a quick peek, enjoying the massive print she wanted in her mouth.

Diesel's thick and strong thigh muscles didn't leave much for her to imagine, even through his work pants. The smoothness of his dark skin made her lick her lips, imagining him tasting like chocolate.

After the waitress took their orders, the wait was long. She ordered a full breakfast of scrambled eggs, grits, hash browns, bacon, Cuban toast, and coffee. Diesel did like grits, although oatmeal was his thing, so he got a hot bowl of that along with a freshly made Cuban fruit smoothie. It was made with guava, pineapple, strawberry, and bananas.

"You always eat that healthy?" she asked, watching him tap his fingers on the table. She wanted him to work them just as hard on her body.

Diesel shifted in his seat, hearing her thoughts that made him cringe. The food couldn't get there any faster. Luckily for him, the waitress approached their table with a tray filled with their food.

"Oh, let me go wash my hands," he said, getting up to head to the restroom. When he did, he stopped and stared, his heart beating erratically.

It was her.

Rose Steel.

Instantly, her usually soft eyes turned into slits followed by a scowl. Diesel was indeed caught off guard but relished in the beauty she still possessed, even with the scowl. She was dressed in her usual, a pair of khaki slacks, a button-down top, and a lab coat. Her hair today, however, was parted down the middle, slicked into two ponytails.

He was fucked, and he knew it, feeling Rose fume. Her eyes quickly dropped down to April's long claws that rested on one of his hands, and his did too.

He pulled away, and April asked, "What?" She knew why he did too, seeing the look on Rose's face as she laughed. "Boy, fuck them college girls. I can make it easier, way easier for you," she said, when in reality, she'd just made it harder.

All those feelings he thought were gone out of his system were now kicking him in the ass.

12

I'm not surprised in the least bit, Rose thought to herself, watching all of April's backside from the front as her gut spilled over her pants at the waist. Of all the places she came to get her father some food, she chose this place, and there he was.

It didn't help that she hadn't heard from him since he fixed her car. He didn't even have the decency to reach out to see if it was still working. She knew they weren't dating, but she was sure they'd made a connection.

Looking straight ahead, Rose decided to ignore him and the trash he'd walked in with as they passed her by. She took a few deep breaths, fighting hard to formulate a complete thought. She was mad, fucking mad, ready to curse his fine ass out.

Working her way through the line, she kept stealing

glances to see if he came out of the bathroom. With a quick glance, they were back at their table, engaged in what she assumed was a lively dialogue based on the woman's reaction.

While she chattered away, she felt his burning eyes on the side of her head. Whatever she was talking about now must didn't interest him, feeling warm. She felt stupid, tugging on her lab coat and khaki slacks while the woman he was with was definitely working hard to be seen.

She'd never judged a woman by what she wore or how she behaved, but she couldn't help standing there with hurt feelings and a bruised ego after the way Diesel made her feel. Struggling to keep it together, she gave his female companion a once over, concluding she had to be easy. Unluckily for her, she wasn't, accepting that ship had came and sailed.

Finally making her way to the front of the line, out of nowhere, it felt as if the air thinned out. She looked to her left and then her right, and there he was right in her space as always. By then, she somewhat knew what she'd wanted. Well, to eat, that is. Good thing she did since he had her mind all scrambled up every time he came around.

"Can I help you?" the woman behind the counter asked as Rose did her best to ignore him.

"Yes, may I have *two* cheese, sweet plantain, and ham sandwiches? Oh, and a cup of espresso and a large orange juice?" Her face was tight, emphasizing the two, and he couldn't help but hear the "fuck you" that came with it once she was done.

Fuck me? Naw, fuck whoever you ordering for.

Diesel wasn't feeling that at all, wondering how long she was going to stand there and pretend he wasn't there. She worked hard to maintain a stern face, looking forward as she hummed as if she didn't have a care in the world.

He laughed, tugging on the end of his nose as he looked around. If he could snatch her little ass up and force her to leave with him he would, but not without incident. She was really getting good at being a brat, but he didn't care. Feeling that same churning he'd felt the night they met, he knew then she was fighting the urge to talk to him.

He even felt it in the warm air swarming around them. It was thick, laying heavily on her skin that was peppered with sweat. He wanted to lick that shit, taste her, and make her pay for disrespecting his presence.

"Espresso is kind of strong and clearly, baby girl, you're hot," he said, then grinned as he stole a glance at her thick ass she laid out for him.

"How much?" she asked the woman, looking through her purse to get her wallet. After fumbling around, she pulled it out but looked up, seeing a twenty-dollar bill he'd slipped on the counter to pay for her food.

"Excuse me, sir, but I got this," she fussed lowly, sucking her teeth.

"How soon do we forget," he whispered in her ear, feeling her body tense up and her thoughts betrayed her. "You know my name...*very well*."

"Anyway, why else would I come in here if I couldn't pay for my own food?" The truth was, she was using her last twenty bucks until she got paid next week without going in her stash.

"Why else?" he asked as he chuckled lowly. "To see me," he said, smiling hard as he felt his nerve endings going into a frenzy.

Everything she was feeling told him she wanted him, she missed him. He could even feel her heart palpitating erratically, even smell her essence that pooled just a little as she shifted when adjusting her book bag. She didn't want to leave it in the car out of fear of someone smashing a window.

With ease and without permission, Diesel slipped his arm behind her back and up her arm, taking the book bag off her shoulder.

"Hey, that's—"

"Yours, I know. It's heavy, Rose and last I checked, you're clumsy as shit."

"Fuck you," she grumbled, crossing her arms as she fought hard not to smile.

"When?" he asked, resting his arm on her lower back. "And you are clumsy, little baby."

To that she snorted while laughing, giving in, but she just couldn't help it. "You say the craziest things," she told him, shaking her head.

When she did, she warmed his heart and ignited the parts of him that no woman had ever touched.

"Mean it too. You forgot?"

"Whatever, Diesel. Thanks for reminding me."

He drew closer, and she let him but still would not look him in the eyes. She didn't have to. He knew she saw him. Hell, he was all she saw, and vice versa. It felt good being next to him, damn good.

Looking down at the space that was closed, Rose sighed but didn't move. She felt anxious, wishing he'd just put her out of her misery and grab her hand, and like that, he did. She let him, too, saying nothing. It was so natural for them to be so in tuned, each feeling like home for the other.

As they waited for her food, he'd forgotten all about April, who was giving him the ugly face. She didn't know who this woman was, but she was messing up her morning shot at Diesel's wood. She'd been trying for two years, and this was the closest she'd gotten.

"I think you're being rude," Rose finally said, looking in April's direction.

"Who? Me?" he said, looking back at her. "Pfft, she works next to the shop," he said with a shrug. "Her and her dude own the pawnshop."

"He knows you're taking his woman out to eat?"

"He doesn't have to, because I'm not, crazy girl. And if it was, why am I here standing with you, holding your hand, your book bag, and paying for you and your nigga's food?" he whispered, tickling her ear.

"It's my daddy's food, sir—I mean, Diesel."

"A'ight," was all he said, hoping she told the truth. He couldn't read her mind sometimes even with his gift because sometimes Rose's thoughts were like a puzzle or blank, telling him nothing at all. Yet, her presence soothing and calming as he kissed the back of her hand.

"It is for my daddy, Diesel. You think I would let you pay for another man's food?"

"Naw, 'cause there won't be another man in the first place," he replied, getting an attitude even talking about it. "Anyway, what's up with Blue? She's running good?"

"Blue," she said and smiled, eyes lighting up. "She's actually running amazing. Whatever you guys did has her running like a new car. I'm still trying to figure out what that is."

He was pleased to hear that, never having to worry about it breaking down anytime soon. Especially after he replaced the entire engine. He didn't do it for anything in return, short of him having peace of mind and her deserving it. She didn't know it, but on that one wet night full of bickering, she'd given him a reason to want to live and love again.

She wrinkled her nose, fanning the air, and he caught it, immediately leaning in to sniff her. The fragrance she wore along with her pussy smelled so good. He wanted to eat her. She looked his way, eyeing him suspiciously.

"What? I stink?"

"Fuck no, girl. Quite the opposite," he said, grinning before he tucked his lips as he imagined her pussy in his mouth.

"You say anything, I swear," she said, feeling warm again. "Whew, it's hot. I wish they'd hurry up."

He wanted to touch her face, wipe her forehead, touch her lips, and swipe her lips with his tongue. He was ready to apologize for shit he hadn't even done yet and would get on one knee in front of all of these people to ask for another shot. Knowing her, she'd let him, but he had a better idea, playing dirty.

Ask me if I want to ride with you, meet your father. We could rap a little about cars and what he thinks about me wanting to wife his baby girl.

Then he remembered he had to get rid of April, who was chewing like a cow, stabbing her eggs and bacon like the food was alive.

April, you realized you left something at home. Get there before it's time to open the store. Take my food and give it Bean. Surprise him. He would like that.

"Hey, you think she would mind if I stole you for an hour or two?" Rose asked as April headed their way.

"Rose, April," he said, immediately introducing them.

"Diesel, I have to go. I left something at the house. And before Bean starts tripping about me opening up late, I need to head out." Then she looked at Rose. "Hey, girl."

"Hi," Rose said watching her size her up.

"Aye, D, you have good taste."

"I do," he said, pulling Rose to him.

"I'll see you later?" she asked Diesel, catching Rose's energy.

"Not today," Rose answered for him. "But it was nice meeting you."

Once April was gone, Rose wasn't too sure she believed their story and Diesel knew it, too, nipping it in the bud.

"Rose," Diesel begged. "Baby girl, just chill and stop overthinking it," he said, slipping into her head. He could easily pretend that he didn't want to listen, but he did. He was tired, tired of the cat and mouse game. He was all in, telling himself that if their paths crossed again, then maybe she was the one.

It was hard for her to stay mad, especially when his presence was intoxicating, willing her to just give in. As she stood there, wondering why and what if as she waited on her food, Diesel went out on a limb, ready to make his plea. It was now or never, and never just wasn't an option. She wanted him, but he needed her.

"Rose, if you plan on dragging my ass because you didn't like how I moved, I get it, but I won't waste your time or mine. It was fucked up, but trust me, it got sticky for me. But after today, I swear if you say we can't move forward, we wont. I'll forever move like we've never met, sweetheart. This some real shit I'm speaking."

"I don't know," she replied even though she did. This was the most alive she'd felt since he last time she saw him.

"Well, I do," he said, taking her book bag off so he could hand it back to her.

When he did, her head snapped quickly his way, eyes shooting daggers at him as his body felt like it was on fire matching the heat in hers. "Keep it and get my food, Diesel. See you in the car."

With that, she took off, pushing the door hard as she went to the car, leaving him by himself.

"I got one at home just like her," the guy behind him said, laughing. "They're nuts, but hey, we can't live without them."

Feeling her resolve give in to him, even as she sat in the car, Diesel felt like the luckiest man in the world. He finally looked love in the face and dared it to make a fool out of him. She agreed to be his now, and that was all that mattered.

13

"Great show tonight," Sheik said to Angelica as she came out of the dressing room.

Tonight, they had a packed house, and Angelica, as always, was the ring mistress who kept the show going in between acts. Being a Moon had its advantages, but it also meant she spent more time being anything but herself since they actually shifted. And when she wasn't herself, she was lethal, dangerous. Especially when Getty would go as long as he had cutting her off.

Sheik, however, had been slated to be hers since they were kids. An arranged marriage wasn't uncommon amongst the Etans. They believed in remaining pure and powerful within each faction, and this was one way of making sure the Moons did.

While everyone felt her "thing" for Getty was over,

Sheik knew better. In due time, Sheik's goal was to eliminate Getty from Etan, and for good. But for now, he played none the wiser as he worked on getting Angelica to love him and only him.

While they fucked regularly, he knew her heart was occupied by her love for someone else, and he hated it. He could feel her spiraling like she was someplace else as they fucked in different forms from cheetahs to wolves.

"It was okay. Exhausting, but okay."

"Well, how many Moons can shape shift into ten creatures and not miss a beat and still look beautiful while doing it?" he asked, coming up behind her as he cupped her ass.

Angelica just wanted to sleep, but it didn't feel like sleep unless it was Getty who'd put her to bed. *It's a lifeline curse,* she supposed, wishing she could rip her own heart out to stop loving and craving him.

She turned and smiled, putting on for Sheik, who looked like he wanted to devour her right then and there. "Not many, but it's why I am who I am."

"So fucking good at it. Let's go eat," he said, taking her by her hand.

The Moons were quite exotic in everything they did. Like wild animals, they were daredevils that enjoyed the nightlife and expensive meals and alcohol.

While Solars were into more natural products and things that grew from the Etan land, the Moons were hunters, enjoying fattened animals that had the most tender meat when compared to those humans ate on Earth.

Still, the Moons were considered the upper echelon faction when compared to the Solars. The other factions weren't as prominent, often remaining amongst themselves, but the fairies weren't a faction. Their existence was sort of unique, often sought out to resolve conflict in Etan, like casting spells, even eliminating plagues. They didn't procreate out of their own, somewhat similar to the Moons, who believed in staying pure. Still, over time, even the fairies had their own who broke their laws and had gone rogue.

Fairies, unlike the Moons and Solars, however, couldn't care less about material things. They lived humbly and without much fuss about what tomorrow held, short of being happy. And while the Moons and Solars were competitive, the fairies never felt the need to compete. Contentment was their strength, never allowing bitterness, jealousy, grief, or strife to shift the course of their design. But make no mistake about it, a fairy, when crossed, was a dangerous one and one that didn't spare life.

The crazy thing was that Diesel had powers similar to the fairies, but he never spoke of them. They figured it had to do with his mother's natural ability to want to help people and be a nurse. His father had been on Earth for only a few weeks, managing to save her life when she was found in an alley brutally beat up. And the rest was history while history seemed to be with secrets that soon could haunt them.

In fact, Etan was full of mystery and secrets, but one thing that wasn't a secret was Sheik's love for Angelica. Cruising through the night air, Sheik couldn't help but steal glances her way. She was like a true black goddess with cheekbones to die for. Her long eyelashes were so long that she could easily take on the form of a butterfly when batting them if she wanted to.

Grabbing her hand, Sheik rubbed it with the pad of his thumb. He would never give up on her, but he had to remind her who she belonged to. "Come here," he told her, tugging her hand just a little.

Sighing, she subtly rolled her eyes but moved toward him anyway.

"Closer."

"Sheik?"

"Closer," he demanded this time, clenching his jaw.

"Fine." When she did, he turned his head toward her, his lips near her ear. "Pull my dick out."

Sheik had been hard since she walked out of that dressing him, but smelling her scent when she scooted over had him really aroused. Sucking her teeth, she tried to pull away until he stopped her.

"So he can, but I can't?"

"Now what is that supposed to mean?" she shot back, now tightly in his grip as he wrapped his right arm around her lower back. “Sheik, baby. Come on, now. Not tonight. This is crazy.”

“No, what’s crazy is you thinking I don’t know you still want that clown.”

“What clown, Sheik?” she grunted.

“Oh, he’s not a real clown because he can’t fucking shift into one? Trust me, he’s a real ass clown, Angelica.” He had to be, Sheik smelling him a few months back at Angelica’s place. He could tell he was all over her, too. To keep from killing her, he ignored it, but Angelica’s continued lying was weighing heavily on him.

“Fuck Getty,” she said, finally saying his name. “He’s a thing of the past, Sheik. Trust me, it’s all about you,” she said seductively, batting those same eyes that pulled him in.

Sheik grunted, tucking his lip before kissing her on the forehead. He decided the lie was necessary to have a good night, which she agreed he assumed as she unzipped his pants and slipped her slender fingers inside.

“We are almost there, but I’d rather do it there,” she whispered, meaning her restaurant.

“I know, baby,” he moaned as she began to work her magic while he stretched his legs. “Did I say I was sorry?” he asked before her mouth replaced her fingers. “Ah, fuck, baby,” he groaned. He was fighting hard not to experience a shift.

Angelica did that to him every time, and this time

was no different.

"Shit, Ang! Shit, shit, shit!" He almost swerved, feeling her lips on the base of his shaft as they touched his lower abdomen area. "Guess you couldn't wait, huh?"

His entire ten-inch dick was down her throat. She moaned, working her tongue up and down, not a tonsil traceable as she stretched the length of her throat to receive all of him.

"Alright! Shit!" he cried out, stopping abruptly out front in the parking lot. "Enough, fuck," he groaned, trying to pry himself out of her mouth.

"Mmmm," she said and smiled, causing him to almost cry it felt so good. There was no fucking way he was letting Getty have her ever. "That was good," she hissed, wiping the lipstick that smeared from around her mouth. Angelica sat up and kissed him on the cheek. "Does that seem like a woman still after another man?" she asked him, her lips on top of his as he tried to gain his composure.

He looked down at semi-erect member, remnants of her saliva still coating it as he shook his head no. Angelica knew what was next, but she went along with it anyway. Sheik enjoyed showing her off, taking her to a spot the Solars frequented. And because it was a Solar restaurant was exactly why it was her favorite.

As soon as they got out, it was as if the paparazzi of Etan was there as they exited his car, smiling and waving at the patrons and staff that held the door for them. All was well until they got in, and Angelica lost her footing.

"Damn, it should be me with the way you just—"

"Angelica, nice seeing you. Sheik, my man. What's up?" Getty asked as the paparazzi shifted their attention to him.

"Uh, nothing. You know, taking the missus out after a kick-ass show. Ang put in some work tonight," he said, bending down and kissing her forehead as he rubbed her shoulders. She felt tense, and she should, but he'd never embarrass her with all eyes on them.

"Yes, she does put on one hell of a show. A damn good one. The last one almost blew me away." Getty laughed, patting Sheik on the shoulder. "Try the sealew. That shit's good. A bottle is easily a few grand, and it's on me. Night, good folks," he said with a smile, walking off as he left Angelica there, shaking like she was about to shift.

"Fucking weak ass shifters," he said, his thoughts then shifting to that of Zara. He already knew Diesel was back into Roseland. That was what he called him, walking around looking goofy and shit. Truth be told, he wished he had someone he could walk around and look goofy for too, peeking back at Angelica.

She looked sad, defeated, and he couldn't care less.

Fuck her and Etan. He was headed back to Earth to clear his head and find Zara.

14

"Spill it," Zara whispered once their professor walked by their lab table.

It was the one lab they did share together, often filled with gossiping as they barely paid attention, but not today. Luckily for Zara, whenever they did, she'd just go home and ask Hugh about something they didn't understand and would then tell Rose.

Today they were studying molecular cells extracted from mice, assessing for abnormalities. The goal was to look at ways abnormal cells influenced their functioning.

While Rose was intrigued, Zara wasn't. She heard about it all the time at home, but she was impressed with how Hugh's research was influencing what the university exposed them to.

Close to falling off to sleep, she yawned and looked Rose's way, who was sitting there grinning sheepishly. She wasn't sure how much she wanted to share about her newfound love interest, but if she did tell anyone outside of her father, it would be Zara.

She was too embarrassed to give her all the details about when they'd first met. And once he sort of went missing for a while, she was glad she didn't. Besides, compared to Zara, what she and Diesel had done was nothing to brag amount. They ate, talked, held hands, and called each other throughout the day, but when they kissed, my God, it was indescribable.

Rose hadn't been fucked for years, short of the toy Zara had given her. Chewing on her nails as she thought about the night before, Rose felt it was time to get a few pointers from her bestie.

"Come here," Diesel grunted, feeling the need to touch her.

His voice was demanding, barely audible, but she heard the urgency in it and felt it too. She took a step each time his index finger drew her his way like a guitar player plucking a string.

Standing there in front of him, Diesel's brown orbs softened, and he smiled. His iced-out teeth shined so brightly, Rose wanted to taste them with her tongue, taking his mouth and tongue into hers.

Reaching for her hand, he pulled her down next to him, dragging her legs across his. "Die—"

"Shhhh, give me your feet."

When she did, he gently her kneaded small circles in her flesh. Rose chewed on the inside of her jaw as she fought to maintain her composure.

Shaking his head to himself, Diesel was adamant he wasn't going to slip inside her head, but her moans and gasps could not be ignored. He pulled on her big toe, tugging it just a little before he grabbed her entire foot and lifted it up. Staring at her clean toenails, he wondered how cute they would look polished.

Cringing, she tried to pull her foot back, but he wouldn't let her.

"Stop it," he told her, then pulled it up to his mouth and kissed it.

"Diesel, don't!" she squealed.

"Shhhh," was all he said, fucking her toes up as he kissed, then sucked on them one by one.

"You like kissing feet?" she asked, eyes rolling in the back of her head as she leaned back.

"Actually no, but I like kissing your feet..." he said, "...and your toes." This time going back to the big one, he pecked it a few times before he lifted her leg, going for her calves.

Rose was getting a kick out of it, watching him peck his way all up her leg until she was flat on her back and he was now on top of her. It happened so fast, she didn't realize it until it happened.

Breathing erratically while his chest was pressed firmly against hers, Diesel was going in for what felt like their first kiss. Sure, he'd sneak in a kiss or there, but this kind of kiss was different. He neared her lips like a yellow light blinking caution, but decided to gun for it anyway.

"Rose Steel?" he said gently in her mouth, tasting something sweet. He wasn't sure what it was, but he liked it. She always was sweet, fruity which matched what he always could be found eating. After a few seconds, he said it again as her mouth hung open, waiting for him to taste her tongue and lips again. "Rose, baby?"

Hearing him call her baby woke her and her center up.

"Yes," she croaked.

"I'm so sorry," he said, dropping his forehead on hers.

Stop it now because once you take it there, that's it, he told himself. As she wound her hips, her center rubbing and bumping against his, he shook his head no while every nerve ending from his fingertips to his toes screamed out yes.

"Why are you sorry?" she asked, searching his eyes as she silently begged him to fuck her.

Just this one time. That's it, and I won't again. Ever, he lied to himself, wrestling with his thoughts. He wanted Rose Steel. All of her. He wanted to lick her, taste her, feel her, fuck her, own her, and devour her. He wanted to consume all of her, so he finally asked.

"Rose, baby? Let me taste you?" he asked, face strained with his eyes closed. He could feel their energy, her yearning, his yearning, tugging back and forth.

He was a big ball of sexual and passionate energy, and

she was reeling him in. Her pussy was belting yes as her essence seeped into his nose, but the good guy in him wanted to be fair and rationale.

"Hmmm," she moaned, overpowering his will. "Yes, please," she groaned.

He'd watched her for nights playing in that pussy, his pussy, never once violating her—if watching her didn't count. By now, he had memorized her scent. It was embedded in his brain. His senses went wild the more he inhaled it.

"You sure?" he managed to get out, kissing her back.

She was so sure that she'd helped herself out of her own bottoms, never once releasing his mouth while their tongues softly tangoed. Diesel had to laugh, but only for a moment after he felt that heat rise between her legs.

"Diesel?" she whispered. She was slowly coming undone, and he hadn't even touched her. "Please?" she begged lowly, followed by a bite and tug on his bottom lip.

"Okay, baby girl." His voice was raspy and rough like his hands that glided as if her skin was silk to touch.

Where he was rough, she was soft. Where he was strategic in his movements, she'd become undisciplined, touching him everywhere. His face, his neck, his chin, his throat.

"Rose, baby." Then it happened when he said her name as she pushed his face all into her pussy. "Shit," he mumbled, greedily licking and tasting her.

Her back arched like a magnet, commanding him to keep going. He was in awe, staring at her pink mound against her dark, slick lips. Her folds separated and bloomed like a flower as he pulled back and spread her legs before blowing into her pussy.

"Diesel!" she cried out, missing the absence of his mouth on her. "Just fucking do it!" His reply was a kiss against her fattened second set of lips, covering her entire pussy with his mouth, sucking it like the sweet peach it was.

"This is sweet... I mean some sweet pussy, Rose," he whispered, making love to it with his mouth.

Like butterflies breaking out of cocoon so they could fly away, so did her center as he chased her release with each suck.

"I can drown in this shit and still come back up for more. Oh yeah, I fucks with this, Rose. I don't care if I never can go back."

"Bitch, did you hear me?" Zara asked her, wondering what the hell was going on.

"Wh—What?" Rose asked.

"Class is over, and you were... hell, I don't know where you were."

Grabbing her by the arm, Zara quickly escorted her out of the lab room, straight to the bathroom. Rose was warm to touch, very warm, scaring her. When they got in there, she locked the door and leaned against it, crossing her arms.

"Now, spill it. What's going on with you? I just asked you what's been up with you, and you totally got all googly-eyed, molesting your fucking bottom lip."

Embarrassed, she lied. "I'm tired, and you're right. I am warm," she said, feeling clammy as her shirt stuck to her chest.

"That's it. I'm taking blood myself later on. I will have Hugh run it because whatever is going on with you is scaring me."

"It's nothing, Zara," she whined.

Zara hated not knowing what was going on with her best friend. They were so close, and now she felt like an outsider. She hadn't even had the chance to tell her that something was off with Hugh, very off. He didn't even want to fuck her as of late.

Feeling bad, Zara retreated as she pulled her in for a hug. "I'm sorry, okay? But Rose, you know you overdo it."

"Nope, nope. I'm fine, Zara."

"Prove it then. Come by tonight and let me take some blood. Hugh has a testing lab there, so it won't cost you anything. Come on, Rosey. I'm scared."

Not much scared Zara, so Rose decided to give in.

"Okay, okay. How about later on before I head to the diner? I can stop by, and once I prove I'm okay when those results come back, I promise to work on getting more sleep and even some exercise."

"Girl, you lose a pound, and those B-cup titties will be in a training bra. So no. No diet. Just slow down, Rose."

Rose's life was anything but slow, and with Diesel around, she was happily spiraling out of control.

15

"Run it back," Getty said, frustrated as he snatched the headphones off his head. He'd been recording this same song for twelve hours. It was called "She Got a Hold on Me", and the truth was, she did. Even though he was tripping off seeing Angelica with Sheik, he was more upset that he reacted.

He didn't love Angelica, but the fact she was stepping out with a Moon he'd been beefing with for years had him hot. He wanted to fuck the daylights out of Zara, but short of that one meeting face-to-face that still had him spooked, he spent most of his time cooped up in the studio. He hadn't even seen his parents, and that wasn't even like him.

"Naw, you know what? Let's call it a night."

"Shoot, more like a day...two days," Tango, his

producer, mumbled as he yawned. He didn't know what was up with Getty, but he was ready to catch some Z's. It was almost one o'clock in the morning.

"Man, fuck you," he said, laughing. "We got this. I just need some rest and pussy," he slipped in as he came out the booth. He dapped Tango up as finished up for the night, but still felt off like he had to get something out. It was so frustrating since music came easy to him.

"Yeah, get some. We got a month to finish up this album. I know you're hot on those charts right now, G, but the fans are waiting. Consistency is key."

"They are waiting for me, huh?" he said, putting on his winning smile with his pretty boy ass. His thick, wavy curls were full now the longer his hair grew, even with the Mohawk shaved clean on each side. They sort of hung to the side, forcing him to push a few out of his face.

Instead of leaving with Tango, he grabbed his guitar and decided to pluck out a tune. It had been gnawing at him for a few days. Whenever he got like that, he knew he was battling something—something he would never admit to anyone, not even Diesel. Deep down he knew that was the need to be in love, to give and receive, too. Without it, Getty was callous and dismissive, and it was fucking with him.

Ironically, while he was in a funk spending the rest of the night alone, Zara was too. Hugh was out of town yet once again, and Rose, with her new secretive self, was at work or somewhere doing God knows what if you asked Zara.

"I want some pizza," Zara mumbled to herself, hopping in her Maserati as she dropped the top down.

It was kind of breezy tonight as she rode down Brickell Avenue in downtown Miami. The couples were out, and sports fans were heading to watch The Heat play at the American Airlines Arena.

Zara loved hanging out and trying new things, but with Hugh's schedule, they didn't get a chance to do it much. Remembering Casolas, a nearby New York pizza spot that stayed open to the wee hours of the morning, Zara decided to grab a slice.

An hour later, Getty wrapped up his session, pleased after he listened to the song he composed a few times before calling it a night.

"Damn, I'm hungry," he said to himself. He could have Grubhub or DoorDash deliver him something, but he was too hungry to wait. "Naw, let me get something on my way home."

Surprised he didn't have a taste for pussy anymore, Getty hopped in his Phantom and turned up the music loud to 99JAMZ, listening to the old-school deejay, Freddie Cruz.

"His old ass be bumping," he said, bobbing his head.

He'd been running the late-night show since Getty

could remember. Tonight, Freddie was playing Blackstreet's version of "Before I Let You Go". Getty loved a good slow jam, admittedly creating provocative and profound lyrics that were jaw-dropping. But truth be told, Getty preferred a love ballad or melody.

"Before I let you go away, can I get a kiss good night?" he swooned lowly as thoughts of Zara crept into his mind as he decided to pull up and go to his favorite pizza spot. When he hopped out, he was eager to get a few slices to hold him over for tomorrow's session that he knew would be long.

When he walked inside, he looked up and thanked the Etan elders or somebody, watching his dream on Earth standing in front of him. It was fucking Zara.

"No staring, creepy guy. Besides, I'm engaged," she sassed, raising her left hand as she wiggled her fingers when she caught him staring with intentions.

"Then tell him he fucked up, leaving you alone then," he told her, checking her out. He knew she had no clue who he was, but tonight was the night. He was going for it.

Her blue and white striped T-shirt hugged her body tightly. Her breasts, full and round, sat up and greeted him nicely while his eyes took a trip down the beautiful canvas of her fat ass and hips.

I want her, even if she is full of herself.

"We are not twins. Can a girl get a little room?" she

quipped, crossing her arms. The line was long, so she had time to play. She would never cheat, but something about him made her want to play.

"Yo, boss man?" he called out to the owner who knew him very well.

"Getty," he sang. "The usual?"

"Yeah, and anything she wants," he said, ignoring the line.

Zara knew that was some boss shit and squinted to remember where she knew him from. Then she did, covering her mouth.

"Oh no. You're him, the singer. Getty Riker," she squealed.

"Shhh... chill, ma," he said, looking around. He liked attention when he was on stage, but when he wasn't performing, he'd rather blend in.

Five hours later, as the sun began to break the sky, Zara and Getty were still sitting there, laughing and eating cold pizza. After Getty paid for the time alone, the owner locked the doors, leaving them inside where they sat like two old friends getting reacquainted.

"I am so going to pay for this," Zara said and laughed, realizing she had to be in class in a few hours.

Getty smiled, dropping his eyes. He'd never paid for pussy, unless paying for Jose to close down the shop counted, but he was fine with that.

Zara was refreshing to him. She had a touch of hood

to her, but he could tell she had a decent upbringing, especially when she spoke fondly of her parents. She loved her mother to no end, which meant she was very much interested in pleasing her mother. And it finally made sense once she told him why she was still with Hugh.

"So why are you able to hang out like this with a fiancé?" he asked.

She shrugged her shoulders, and then said, "He's out of town working."

"And didn't take you with him?" he probed, fighting not to touch her.

Truthfully, her conversation and energy were so enticing, sex hadn't even crossed his mind. He just wanted to treat her like they were on a date, doing what couples did, which was holding hands and stealing quick kisses across the table from each other.

"Naw. Conferences and research. He raises a lot of money for the university hospital, money for research and hopefully, successful treatments. He loves what he does, and I love how passionate he is about medicine."

"Seems like you do like—I mean, love him," he said, hoping she was telling the truth.

Being in love and away from the one you wanted had the tendency to fuck with you. To him, she seemed more bored than sad or alone. Not a woman in love missing her man.

"I know I care about him a lot and love him as a person," she said, embarrassed as her face grew beet red since this was her fiancé she was speaking about. "Ugh, I feel like such a bitch right now telling you that. You must think I'm a loser, a bitch with no heart."

"You have a heart," he said, this time seductively as his eyes traveled down to her breasts perched up nicely for him to indulge in. "I can tell you love hard, and you're loyal too. So, your mother?" he asked, picking up something about their relationship earlier. Besides, he gave no fucks about her man. He wanted to know more about her. "Tell me more about her."

Zara sighed. She did love her mother, but the side she was holding back had to do with the hold her mother had on her. It was disgusting if she were being honest. The seed planted when she was just a teenager. She wasn't even interested in boys or cognizant as to how pretty she was until the day her mother forced her to be. She shuddered thinking about it, and what Getty saw, made him angry.

"No plans this evening?" Rebecca asked her daughter.

She was blossoming into a beautiful, young woman. Her brother was already headed out, and she heard him and his friends make plans for a house party.

"I have plans. See?" she said, holding up a book. It was Kimberla Lawson Roby's latest, The Reverend's Wife.

The smirk was her response, making Zara feel stupid.

She couldn't understand why that was so bad. Most sixteen-year-olds were out drinking and being wild, but not her. She'd been waiting for six months for this book to come out. Her daddy, Richard, brought it home, slipping it on her desk before she came home.

Looking behind her, Rebecca came inside her room and closed the door. "Zara, honey, let's talk," she said, smiling as she sat next to her.

Zara wasn't used to this one-on-one from her mother, but she actually perked up. She didn't receive much attention or affection from her, so whenever she got it, she was like a little child being told they were going out for ice cream after months of not getting any or ever.

"Okay, Mommy," she said, sitting up as she pushed her glasses on her nose. Zara was beyond blind and hated contacts. They made her eyes itchy.

Patting right where she sat, she motioned for Zara to sit next to her. When she did, they were in front of her mirror. "Look at us."

When Zara did, she smiled. They looked so much alike. Almost like sisters, short of her mother's fuller figure and more mature look in terms of hair and makeup.

"I see," she said, then looked at her mother, wiggling her nose.

"It's the glasses. I know what you said, but I think you try the contacts again. And the hair...oh, Zara, it's gorgeous, except it's in this ponytail," she said and sighed. "Imagine if you wore it out, long and full or even straight. People die to

have this hair," she said of Zara's fine hair, given her father's Creole background.

He was half French and spoke it as well. He and Zara's mother met when he was off the ship in town, coming in to grab a few items he wanted to take back home. She'd been staying with her aunt for the summer and working at the bakery where they sold the infamous New Orleans beignets. They made them on the ship, but nothing like the real ones in the city.

"Yeah, but that takes so much time," she complained, then stopped, watching the look on her mother's face.

"You know what takes even more time?" she asked, laying Zara's head down on her shoulder. "Minimum wage pay. Working ten to twelve hours, slaving to make ends meet. I've done it," she said with regret, praying her daughter would never have to.

"Really? When?" Zara couldn't remember a time her mother worked.

She was quite the hostess, though if parties counted. She even gave them the best birthday parties. They were the talk of the town.

"Oh, long before your time. Then I met your father, girl." She laughed, tossing her head back.

Zara felt loved, sharing this moment with her. She wrapped her arms around her mother's waist, holding her tightly. "Tell me more. I want to know all the details."

And when her mother did, the lesson she learned that day was to use what you have to get it all. All, meaning anything that came from the labor of a man—even while laying on your back.

"Damn," Getty said more to himself as Zara shrugged her shoulders once she told him about that night.

She wasn't a known whore, but guys who approached her once her mother helped her intensify her natural beauty automatically knew they couldn't approach her empty-handedly. The sad part about it was Zara was anything but superficial. She actually wanted to specialize in plastic surgery. Mostly burn victims, but she'd even consider others who struggled with their self-worth with the right counseling in place. Getty could tell she meant it too, smiling as she spoke about her dreams.

"So if you don't want to talk to me again, hey, I get it."

"What the hell?" he said and laughed. "Girl, relax. I'm a whole hoe out here, and you're working to change lives, making it happen. I love that shit," he confessed with a smile.

"Oh yeah?"

"Fuck yeah," he said and grinned.

"And why do you seem proud of being a *whole hoe*?" she said, laughing when she emphasized the "whole hoe" part.

"Not proud, just honest. It is what it is. I do want to change, do some different shit. Fuck only one woman. Hell, change her life and make her have my babies."

His delivery was blunt, crass even, but it was undeniably honest just like he said he was. Zara had spent the last few years being everything but honest, so she had no room to judge him.

"Whatever," she replied and smiled, then turned around, giving him her backside as she stood up to dump their trays.

"So that's my cue, I see."

"You can stay, but I have a date with a pillow or, at least, I'm trying to," she said with a yawn.

"My days and nights all blend in," he said, getting up, too. "So put me on your schedule later."

"I did tell you I had a fiancé, Mr. Riker."

"Moore. It's Getty Moore." He had no clue why he was telling her that, but he wanted to hear her say it.

"Getty Moore. So Riker is just what? For entertainment purposes only?" she asked, grabbing her purse.

"It is, but get used to saying it," he told her, walking up to her as he closed the space in between them.

"And why is that?" Zara was nervous.

Getty did something no man had ever been able to do once she understood the power a woman had and not only between her legs.

"Because I'ma change your name, Zara. Let me do that for you?"

"When?" she asked him, giggling.

"Just follow me," he said, grinning like a goofy.

And without fighting it, once he turned around and locked the door, he took her hand, and she let him as he walked her to her car.

"Don't fake me out now. Get in your ride and just follow me."

16

"Hey, babe," Zara greeted Hugh as soon as he walked in the door.

She and Getty had been chatting and texting throughout the day, but no matter what he offered, she decided to friend zone him. Something told her something happened that night she couldn't remember, but she really didn't want to. She was always told it was best for the man to love and want you more. With Getty, that would never happen, so she decided to cut her losses, playing it safe with Hugh.

"Hey, yourself," he said, going in for a kiss as he lifted her up. "Miss me?"

"So much," she lied, her mouth still on hers.

"I missed you, too. Conference was great, donors showed up, and I think I have some leeway on my research," he said and smiled, eager to prove to the hospital he was better than Dr. Lee... and Dr. Kemp.

"That's wonderful, babe. I'm so proud of you," she genuinely replied as he lowered her down, both feet now on the floor.

"Smells good in here."

Zara, feeling guilty about all the time she'd been giving Getty, rushed home right after class and cooked dinner. She wasn't as good of a cook as her mother, but a part of her training from her mother, if you called it that, was her knowing how to feed a man more than pussy. He had to eat food, too.

"Oh, I made your favorite," she told him, taking him by the hand.

Hugh shook his head and smiled. He had no clue what had gotten into her, but he liked it. He also liked the black tights and sports bra she was wearing too.

"We have lamb with white sauce," she gloated, lifting the lid. "Asparagus, garlic mashed potatoes, and for dessert, key-lime pie."

"Wow, guess I need to hurry and shower, and then we can get to—"

"Oh, baby. I forgot," she said, cutting him off. She knew he was about to refer to sex, and to her, that was a given, so she felt no need in faking that she was excited about that. "I need you to run some blood work on Rose. She hasn't been feeling well. Forgetful, warm, just... I don't know."

"Oh yeah? When is she coming into the hospital? I can get Dr. Casey, my assistant, right on it."

"I drew it myself. Left and labeled it in your lab downstairs in the refrigerator."

Hugh wasn't too keen with her going down there when he wasn't home, but she rarely did, so he let it go.

"Playing doctor already?"

"No." She laughed. "I just drew blood. And I am going to be a doctor someday, so nothing is wrong with a little practice," she said seductively, hoping that he gave her some head before dinner. That, along with a glass of wine, would make sex with him at least somewhat enjoyable.

"Let me take a shower. We'll eat, and then I'll get right on it. Deal?"

"Deal." She kissed him once more and headed toward the kitchen.

Hugh was exhausted, but watching his young tiger prance around was just what he needed to unwind and indulge in some good food and pussy.

After hours of getting his fill between her legs, Hugh hopped up to go to his lab. He was still excited about his possible discovery but careful not to share it with others too soon.

Dr. Casey was sharp, jumping in with ease as she quickly became an asset to his research. While his heart was broken about Agnes, Hugh felt it was his karma for not following his heart. He'd be lying if he said he didn't want to go on this journey with Agnes, but he knew his chance of combining his love with medicine and his love for her was beyond repair.

"Now, let me see what's going on here," he said to himself, taking the vial of blood out.

Within an hour, he finished the complete blood count test, cholesterol test, kidney and liver functioning test, blood sugar test, and just for the heck of it, an enzyme marker test. Enzyme marker tests were for people at risk for cancer. All he was doing was waiting for the results.

Afterward, he went back to his notes, cross-checking information he found to update his research notes. By the time he was done, the fatigue he had earlier was back. Not wanting to hear Zara's mouth, which annoyed him sometimes since she was spoiled, Hugh decided why not check the results so he could get a good night's rest and sleep in late. No one was expecting him, and Zara would be out and off to school.

Pulling up to his lab table, he started to study the blood results one by one. Short of her iron and vitamin D being low, he was stumped about what had Zara so riled up. He knew she was overprotective of Rose, too overprotective at times. He had one more test to check before he called it a night—the enzyme markers. And when he did, he nearly passed out.

"Whoa, whoaaa," he said to himself, smiling before he stood up and cheered. "This is..." he said, leaning over and looking at the results again. "This is fucking amazing. I—I need more. More blood," he said quickly, sitting down as he logged on his computer.

Before then, he'd hit wall after wall with no true breakthrough short of some research Dr. Casey brought to his attention this past trip. Being a hematologist, her exposure regarding the study of blood and various diseases was fascinating. Many cancers over the years had been treated with products consisting of blood like bone marrow, so her insight about hematology was perfect, beautifully weaving itself right into his research.

While she was no Dr. Kemp, Dr. Casey was just as dedicated, if not more. As soon as she found out he had a slot available to work on his research, she immediately applied. After reviewing his research proposal, his interest in molecular cell regeneration using various blood samples not only sparked her interest but led to her practically begging him to bring her on board.

As he compared the results to others he'd collected over the years, Hugh felt a high like none other. This was brilliant. Excited, he reached for his cell and stopped, disappointed he couldn't call the only one person whose voice he wanted to hear—Dr. Agnes Kemp.

His chest tightened, and his heart ached, dying to call her. This moment would be beyond perfect if she could share in his excitement. He cringed thinking of her and Dr. Lee, probably laughing every time they got together at the expense of his torn heart.

Hugh was a shameful a mess. When alone, he'd read the text messages between him and Agnes as often as he could and listen to her voice messages throughout the day. Walking past her without her glancing his way felt like death each time, dying only to be revived to die again. He was ashamed, truly ashamed that his need to impress and be validated by others was the cause him to lose the one woman that completed him.

In a moment of desperation, he grabbed his cell, anxious to shoot her a text. He was too prideful to call, uncertain of how he would react if Dr. Lee was around or worse—answered her cell. Agnes had a sexual appetite like no other, leaving him famished since Zara wasn't much of a sex fiend in their bedroom. But Agnes was more than sex to him. She'd become his best friend.

"Hugh, man," he said to himself, sighing. "You got to let it go. Just let it go. You have a beautiful woman in your bed that's yours, all yours. Don't fuck that up, or you will lose out."

Even with that speech, he still wasn't convinced that he didn't have at least one shot at getting back in Agnes's good graces. She was his biggest cheerleader, and most of what he had done was also her work. There was no way him sharing this wouldn't at least open the door to just talk... and maybe more.

"I know what I will do," he said, going to Edible Arrangements' website.

Agnes loved fruit. She quickly devoured it. He'd set up a meeting, a fake meeting, using the university's schedule portal, blocking it off where only she would see it. That, along with a few other things he knew she would appreciate, would be the perfect way to tell her what a dumb fuck he was and that he wanted his best friend back. If she was open to that, maybe, just maybe, he could win her heart back too.

He concluded, as he was on the brink of a treatment-changing medical discovery, that Zara was young, vibrant, and honestly, just not that into him. She might have liked him, even cared for him, but he was a smart man, knowing long ago that what they had wasn't what he needed or her.

He'd faked it long enough, and this was the one opportunity he knew God must have given him to make it right, but first, he needed more blood. To get that, Zara had to stick around just a little bit longer. She had to, without him sharing just why, and it was simple since Rose was her best friend.

"Now, I need to reach out to Dr. Casey. I won't be able to sleep until I do," he said after ordering the arrangement and scheduling the meeting.

One thing he had discovered about Dr. Casey was she rarely slept. He wasn't sure how she managed to put in the hours that she did, but anytime he needed her or logged on to his computer, he would have at least one message from her.

As predicted, when he called, Dr. Casey answered on the second ring.

"Hugh? Is everything okay?" she asked, nibbling on a cookie as she watched one of her favorite movies, *The Purge*. Dr. Casey was weird like that, but anything that was gory and showed lots of blood excited her. Halloween was her favorite day of the year, and she was the first to help the university with their masquerade gala and haunted houses for the students.

"Yes, it's better than okay. I can tell you're up," he said and laughed, shaking his head.

"I am," she said, laughing. "You know me so well."

"I know enough to know you operate off of cookies and research. I still wonder how you never seem to gain any weight."

Dr. Casey was extremely fit. She was of average height and stature for a woman—not lean, but not heavy either. Like most doctors, she kept her hair simple at work, wearing a tight bun that rested at the nape of her neck. Occasionally, when he saw her outside of work, she'd wear it down in a shoulder-length bob.

She didn't date at all to his knowledge, although he felt she was very dateable with a mahogany-colored complexion, big and round sienna-brown eyes, and thin lips that curled when she smiled along with her eyes.

"It's genetics. Thank my parents."

It was funny she'd said that since Hugh had never even met her parents. Not even any of her relatives. Dr. Casey wasn't from the Miami area, but he'd never even heard her mentioning them coming to visit. With an internal battle and skeletons of his own, Hugh kept talk of personal life to a minimum. He went there with Agnes, which led to his mistake, but if he could do it all over again, he still would. He'd just break things off with Zara first.

"Yeah, stop eating and go check out the email I sent you. Hurry," he told her, making her smile.

She loved medicine just like movies, pausing so she could see what had him so wired besides the research she'd already brought him this past week. She eagerly got up, slipping on her house shoes and robe. As she made her way to her laptop, she put on her glasses and logged on. As she entered her password for her emails, Hugh continuously rambled on and on about what this could mean for the medical community, especially cancer patients. When she clicked on the attachment with the test results, she damn near choked.

No fucking way, she thought to herself.

Dr. Casey, like Hugh, could barely contain herself.

"Hugh, where did you get this from?" she asked, moving quickly through a few other documents she had saved on her desktop.

Not only was this something that was needed for

their research, but it might just might be what she needed to deal with something from her past.

"And who is Rose Steel?"

"Never mind that. How soon do you think you can make it into the university hospital in the morning? I know we had a long week, but I can barely contain myself," he said, pacing back and forth, confident he couldn't go to sleep now.

Staring at her two cats, Dr. Casey chuckled. "Well, TeeTee and Taco aren't too happy. They are glaring at me. They've been in the pet kennel all week."

"Fine, I can come to you, but I need to stop by the hospital first. Delilah, do you really know what this means?" he asked, calling her by her first name.

"I think I do. Was the donor ill? Did she complain of any specific symptoms I need to know about?" she asked, studying the other documents she located like a madwoman.

"Not sure, but we can't say anything right now. No word of this please, Delilah. I finally got that fucker," he rejoiced as he beamed, thinking of his victory over Dr. Lee.

I think I finally got the fucker, too. And I bet this Rose Steel can lead me right to Diesel.

While Hugh and Delilah rejoiced although for different reasons, Diesel sat dumbfounded staring at his best friend who looked like he was about to shit on himself.

"So, G, tell me again what you and Zara ran off and did?"

Getty sighed, feeling fucked up yet happy at the same time. He knew it was wrong but after the night he and Zara had, he just had to make her his. He felt guilty once he did it, but as of late, he decided to help her end things with Hugh. Besides, she wasn't in love with him anyway.

"We got married," he said, casually as he shrugged his shoulders. "Flew out to Vegas and just did it. She just don't remember."

To Be Continued

www.ingramcontent.com/pod-product-compliance
Ingram Content Group UK Ltd.
Pitfield, Milton Keynes, MK11 3LW, UK
UKHW022024190726
13853UKWH00005B/2098

9 798556 56612